A Stingray Christmas

Arlie Undercover: Book One

USA Today Bestselling Author

Dani Haviland

Undercover Detective Arlie Biggar had only seen the woman who bore his son five years ago on video. Should he tell her he was the father of her son? Now that they were in danger, he'd move from Alaska to Arizona to protect them…without letting them know who he was.

Dedicated to all those who serve others, whether protecting us at home or abroad, helping with Project Literacy, distributing food to the community, or simply holding a door for someone with two toddlers and an armload of groceries. Thank you!

Chapter 1
Bank Robbery

News Item:

A bank robbery of a different sort occurred in Anchorage Tuesday night when someone broke into the Miracles Happen Sperm Bank and Fertility Center. The company's server was stolen. No 'deposits' were harmed in the break in, but all data files were compromised. The investigation continues.

***

"Hey, Arlie, how's it going?"

"Who's this?

"Ah, Arlie, don't you remember me? Your old pal Jake?"

"I knew I shouldn't have picked up when it said unknown caller. I have nothing to say to you. Good-bye."

Ring! Ring! Ring!

"Who is this and how'd you change my ring tone?"

"Now, don't hang up, Arlie. I really need to talk to you about something important. It may be a matter of life or death."

"You're still the same old drama queen, Jake. What do you

want? You have ten seconds."

"First, I'm sorry for stealing your girl, and I should have apologized a long time ago…"

"Ancient history. Now you have five seconds."

"All right, all right! Geez! It's just that I think someone's trying to kill me. I think it has something to do with that time you used my name when you went to the sperm bank."

Arlie grinned as he recalled the practical joke he had played on Jake when they were still friends, then realized what Jake had just said. "Trying to kill you? Over spunk? What? Did they want more and you wouldn't put out?" Arlie started laughing at his own joke, then realized that Jake hadn't laughed or said anything.

"Are you serious, Jake? Someone's trying to kill you? Why? And how come you think it has anything to do with a college prank, what, seven or eight years ago?"

"I don't know if you heard it on the news, but there was a break-in at that sperm bank. Stop laughing. This is serious. The next day, I got a freaky phone call, asking if I was Jake Spinelli. When I asked who was calling, he got belligerent. 'Either you are or you aren't. Just tell us the truth and we'll have this over in no time.'"

"Sounds like one of your pranks coming back on you. Are you sure it wasn't your little brother?"

"Nah. This guy had a thick Sicilian accent. Or Italian or something like that. And he said, 'us' and 'we'll,' like it was gang-related or something. Anyhow, I said yes, I was Jake Spinelli. He said he found a wallet with my ID in it and wanted to return it to me. Well, I smelled a rat. I don't even carry a wallet, just fold cash over my drivers license and credit card. I agreed to meet him at the mall in the food court in an hour. I told him I'd be wearing a neon green t-shirt so he could recognize me. What an idiot! If he really did have my wallet, he could just look at the photo on my drivers license and know what I looked like.

"So, I wore a button-up black shirt and running shoes, just in case I had to get the heck out of there in a hurry. Wouldn't you know it, some teenage kid goes into the food court wearing the brightest neon green shirt you ever saw. This burly dude with blue-black hair and the biggest, thickest mustache I ever saw went over to the kid and grabbed him by the neck. I don't think he was trying to choke him, but he was lifting him up to his eye level to look him over.

"That poor boy—he couldn't have been more than sixteen

or seventeen—literally pissed himself in fear. I guess I'd have done the same thing at that age if some big Mafia-looking guy grabbed me by the neck. Shoot, I woulda done it today if he had found me. I slid over to the escalator, forcing myself not to run. I was sweating bullets, for sure."

"So, why do you think it has to do with the sperm bank?" Arlie asked, his dry tone letting Jake know that he thought he was crazy.

"Well, I overheard him telling his buddy who was with him—he was just about as big and ugly—that this couldn't be the one because he didn't have red hair and brown eyes and besides, he wasn't old enough."

"Well, you're safe I guess because you're not the one with red hair. I am. And if by some wild ass coincidence this does have something to do with my 'donation,' the only way they'll link me to you is if you say something. Now, I'd like to say it's been nice reconnecting, but you're still just as weird as ever."

"Arlie," Jake said softly, "They said they'd kill the bastard that sired the boy and then get the mother and son, too."

Chapter 2
Shot, but not killed

Anchorage, Alaska
December 15

News item June 21: Two men were arrested today in connection with a year-long investigation into identity theft and money laundering. Anchorage Police Officer Charles Baggar was wounded when the suspects, brothers Alonzo De Luca and Luca De Luca, opened fire. US Marshal Marc Audie returned fire, wounding Alonzo and saving the life of the wounded Baggar who is now listed in critical condition.

***

"Hey, boss," Arlie said. "It's been six months since those bastards shot me. I'm sick and tired of using this cane. It wasn't too bad on dry ground, but I just about wiped out yesterday three steps away from the front door. You know how scary it is walking on fresh snow on top of a sheet of ice. Imagine doing that with a cane. Winter weather sure makes it hard to stay upright. The doc told me if I fell just right—or I guess that would be just wrong—that bullet would nick my spinal cord and I'd be crippled for life. I hate to take a medical leave, but it's either spend winters in Arizona, or I'll have to quit completely and take full disability. Human Resources offered it to me, but…"

"Yeah, I know. Cop blue runs through your veins. I know you don't care for your desk job, but I've never heard you complain." Captain Fergusson stood up and looked around the office. "I think we have enough warm bodies around here to cover the caseload. If you don't mind, though, could we keep you on as a consultant? It wouldn't be much money, but with your sick leave, you could be sitting pretty."

"I'd rather not be on retainer, just in case I get a life in Arizona and want to stay there, but you can call me and I'll give my advice for free. I'll even throw in a few hours of cyber sleuthing if that's what you need. Just don't count on me as one of the team."

"All right, but make sure you give me your new contact info. Are you going to be using an alias? If the charges on Alonzo don't stick, you'll be the first head he goes hunting. He sure hates you for some reason."

"Nah, I'll use my real name. I could kiss that reporter for intentionally spelling my last name wrong."

"And the editor for squelching any corrections that came

in," the captain said, rising to shake the hand of one of the best detectives he'd ever had work for him. "So, Charles Biggar, you're going to be a snowbird, then?"

"Nope. But Arlie Biggar will be. I don't think he's ever heard me called that. He always just called me Daywalker. Now, if you don't mind, I'll finish up both cases I have, turn them over to Trudy so she can review and file them, then I'm online to book a flight to Phoenix. I kinda got started a little early. I…um…already reserved a little trailer for six months. I'll be a Mesan and a Mason!"

"You and you're puns, Arlie. We'll miss you, but you're right. I'd rather know you're safe and able to get around— even if you do have to use a cane—than in a wheelchair or motorized scooter. Grab some fresh fruits and veggies for me and send them up Goldstreak. It'd be worth a trip to the airport."

"I'll do that."

***

"Sorry to leave you without a roommate, but I haven't been much good for anything around here," Arlie said, using his cane to pull his plaques off the top shelf.

"Here, let me help," Nate said. "Don't worry about leaving

me in a lurch. I've been trying to get Natalie to move in here with me for ages. Her lease runs out at the end of the month. She was leery of sharing a two-bedroom one-bath apartment with two men. Now she doesn't have an excuse. She's fussy about sharing expenses, too. She wants to help carry the load, so I won't be losing a nickel. Plus, now I can have sex whenever I want!"

"Yeah, rub it in. You know how long it's been for me? No, don't answer that. I *hope* you don't know. But you do know it's been at least six months. Recovery sucks, plus any 'intimate activities' as the doctor put it, might move that bullet. Why couldn't I have been shot in the arm or chest or just about anywhere else? I feel like Ironman, on the verge of death, with a bullet close to my spine instead of my heart. Well, I guess I wouldn't die, but being a complete cripple would suck. Too bad they don't have some fancy electronic device that could pull this sucker out. Even sneezing scares the bejeezus out of me."

"Let's hope the heat helps with your aches and pains. Sunshine, swimming pools, women running around in bikinis…"

"Ah, shut up, Nate. It's still winter there. Even if it gets in the 60's and 70's, most of the folks in east Mesa are in their 60's and 70's. I don't think I'd care to see little old grannies in bikinis."

"Yeah, well, I've been there in the winter. You'll still see plenty of tanned and wrinkled skin because most of the old folks run around in shorts and tank tops. Now, all I want is for you to get better. Maybe you'll get a Christmas miracle and that bullet will work its way out."

Nate grabbed the tote and set it by the door. "I'll put this box of stuff in storage with mine. I think you had the right idea, selling or giving away replaceable items and just holding on to your memorabilia. No muss, no fuss, no baggage."

"Or packing, unpacking, and moving boxes... Besides, I'll need a completely different wardrobe there." Arlie wrapped his plaques in newspaper and handed them to Nate to put in the plastic tote. "So, you'll still be able to take me to the airport at ten tonight, right? I know the flight doesn't leave for a few hours after that, but I don't want to inconvenience you any more than I already have."

"We're good. I can't imagine going out of town with nothing more than a water bottle and a wallet to carry."

"Well, Nate, I'm looking for a fresh start. You can't do that if you bring old garbage to the game."

***

Arlie had never met either of the women who had purchased the sperm he had deposited using Spinelli's profile, but he knew their names. One had disappeared off the radar before he found out if she had a boy or a girl, but he did know she got pregnant. Maybe she miscarried and moved away because of a broken heart. He didn't know and—according to the papers he had signed with a false name—he had no legal right to know. He had no reason to meet them, and didn't intend to, but he was still fascinated by them. Now that he had the opportunity, though, he'd move closer to the mother of the one who had birthed a son.

Curiosity was both his talent and his curse. It was why he was so good at what he did. He could untangle or create a computer program or app, depending on what was needed. Tying into security cameras worldwide was a cinch to him. He used his skills when needed, but never shared them. There were other governmental agencies that could and did do the same thing. Maybe they could do it from a smartphone, too. No one was saying. And he wasn't asking.

Arlie took out his phone and looked at the app again. She was still at work in the crafts department at Sprawl-Mart. He clicked on the views from the other cameras in the store. Cool! It looked like they were shorthanded. A part time job shouldn't be too hard to get during the Christmas shopping season. He pulled up the resume he used when he was working undercover, changed the names, then saved the file as 'Arlie Biggar-Mesa.' While he was waiting for his connecting flight in Portland, he'd call the contacts who covered as his former employers and let them know about his new alias and job experiences.

He was mesmerized by Charlene. She was and always had been a single mother. No men had been in her life since she signed up for the Mommy Brigade. All things considered, she was stable. She had lost her job as a legal aide in Phoenix two years ago, but didn't take it lying down. The discrimination suit was still pending. After money for lawyers ran out, she took over and filed her own paperwork. She knew what she was doing. The firm she was suing had more money than she could ever think to have. They were playing the waiting game. Delays, appeals, whatever it took, they threw at her. Even if he didn't know hearing dates beforehand, he would have known about them the day afterwards. She always showed up back at her job at Sprawl-Mart but didn't look the same. She still had her inherent good looks, but her spirit was withered, her face pinched in a miserable blend of anger, frustration, and sadness.

By now, she was sure to have spent any cash she had managed to save. He knew her investment portfolio had been cashed out within six months of leaving the law firm. Her job at Sprawl-Mart didn't pay much. The day after her paychecks were direct deposited, she paid bills online. Unless she happened to get overtime, it took one full paycheck to cover her rent. Two to three times a year, when the bi-weekly payments lined up just right, she had a three-paycheck month. She must be putting some of it aside—probably as cash stuffed in a baggie in the freezer. He'd never seen evidence of irresponsible spending, so those dollars were somewhere. She was living on the edge, one major disaster—a blown car engine, uncovered medical expense, whatever—from bankruptcy. And from living in her station wagon with his son.

Carla, the other mother, had dropped off the radar two months after she had been inseminated. He was curious and continued to search for her at least once a week, but if she—and the child she may or may not have carried to term—were still alive, they were probably living in another country. He was good at searching, but even the best had trouble penetrating records in Third World countries.

Chapter 3
A Fresh Start

Post in Mesa Tribune: Now Hiring! East Mesa Sprawl-Mart is now hiring. Bring your resume or apply online at ….

***

"Thank You, Lord, thank You, Lord, thank You!" Arlie said under his breath, then shut the newspaper and grabbed his phone. "New job opportunity for recently re-located stocking clerk and outdoor sports specialist. They're sure to have an opening in one of those departments."

Arlie pulled up the website, keyed in all the required info, added one of his 'safe' social security numbers, then hit submit. "I'll play fair for now. If I don't get hired the first go around, there's always the fun way."

The small park model trailer, or modular as some folks called it, was just the right size for him. A few bucks spent at Sprawl-Mart on the necessities—a coffee maker with mug, granola bars, towels, t-shirts, socks, and shorts—and he was set.

Hmm. I may have to go back and buy some long pants and another pair of shoes. Maybe this time Charlene won't be on lunch break. She looks so much different now from that hard-working law clerk I first saw on the security cameras at her law firm six years ago. Watching her belly grow, day by day. Waiting for her to get back to work after maternity leave… Seeing Chip's bright red hair the first time she took him shopping without that confounded car seat cover over his head. Then the scowls of agony and frustration after being let go because the firm denied her family leave time when Chip got sick.

It had been a long two years, hunting security cameras in her neighborhood, hoping to get a peek at the two of them on the way to doctors' appointments. He sighed and smiled. And how great it was when she got the job at Sprawl-Mart. He could see her for hours on end, five and sometimes even six days a week while working. Too bad there weren't any cameras around her apartment complex. The neighbor who watched Chip never left the area. He hadn't seen the boy for two years until he started school, and then it was random sightings and at low resolution.

"Today, maybe I'll be able to see her in the flesh. And then, one of these days, I'll be able to see Chip, too," he said out loud, hoping to speak his wish into existence.

"Congratulations, Arlie. With your experience, we'd like to hire you as an assistant manager, but unfortunately—for you, that is—we promote from within. I'm afraid you'll have to start at the bottom like the rest of us did. Right now, the only opening in sporting goods is for someone to assemble bicycles. Would you be willing to do that?" Seth, the twenty-something year old associate asked.

"Would you be my boss?" Arlie asked, trying to suppress a grin.

"Yes, sir, I would. Does my age bother you? Would that be a problem if I asked you to do something?"

"Nope. Not at all. I just wanted to make sure I knew who to ask if I had a question."

Seth's scrawny shoulders relaxed visibly. Evidently, his youth had been a problem in the past. "I'll have human resources contact you. We have a few other applicants, but I'm hoping they choose you. All I can do is suggest, but you're my number one choice."

Arlie stood up and shook the youth's hand. "It's been a pleasure, Seth. I look forward to hearing good news from HR soon."

Arlie left the meeting with a spring in his step that he hadn't felt since before he'd been shot. *That's a lie! It's been longer than that!*

Arlie sighed as he realized his inner voice was letting him know that he was blaming all his miseries on the shooting. Yes, it felt great to be a cop and be of service to mankind, even if as a whole, law enforcement officers weren't appreciated. *But what you really want is to be of service to a woman, and that ain't gonna happen without a miracle.*

"Crafts," Arlie said aloud to silence his inner conflict. He walked up and down the aisles, looking for something that might spark his creative interests enough that he'd need to ask Charlene a question. Maybe he could buy yarn and learn to knit or crochet. That would be fine if he was in Alaska, but who needed a scarf in the desert?

And there it was. Pillow forms. He really did want a throw pillow or two for the couch.

"May I help you find something, sir?"

"Oh, no. I mean, yes," Arlie stammered at hearing Charlene's voice for the first time. He took a deep breath to compose himself.

"Sorry, I didn't mean to startle you."

"No, no, I'm fine. It's just I want a couple throw pillows, but the ones in home décor are, well…"

"Ugly?"

"Yeah, very ugly. I don't own a sewing machine, but I guess these plain white ones are better than those other ones."

"I'll tell you what you can do to cover these without using a sewing machine. You'll need a good pair of scissors and a straight edge, though. And a steady hand, but you're pretty young. Some of the older folks who come in here have the shakes so bad, I'm afraid to let them walk out with a pair of scissors, even in the cardboard package! Come look at this fabric. Which one do you like?"

"How about this one?" Arlie said, choosing a Navajo print polar fleece.

"That's a good one. Now, what size pillow?"

He pulled one off the shelf and handed it to her. "Now what?"

Charlene grabbed the bolt of fabric and set it on the cutting table. "Hand me the pillow."

Arlie gave her the pillow and watched as she measured across the face of the pillow from edge to edge with a cloth tape measure. "See, the bag says twelve inches for the size, but measured across the loft, it's actually sixteen inches. Add five inches to each side and you'll need two thirty-six by twenty-six-inch pieces of fabric for a cover." Arlene proceeded to show him how to mark out the sixteen by sixteen 'no-cut zone' in the middle of the square piece of material, then cut five inches into it, making a fringe. "Just make sure you have a good pair of scissors. Then all you do is start tying square knots. Make sure you put the pillow in the center before you do the last side, though, otherwise you'll spend more time untying your knots."

"Which are the best scissors?" he asked, trying to keep the inner glow he was feeling from leaking out as a flirtatious grin.

"These are the best. I got a pair when I was in high school. They'll still cut through multiple layers of fabric, even though they've never been sharpened. These are good, too. Probably good enough for a casual seamstress..." Charlene looked him in the eye and winked, "or tailor."

"I'll take these," he said, and pulled the more expensive chrome-plated ones off the rack. "I like shiny objects. Who knows? I might have just found a new career path."

"Well, if you need anything else, just ask."

"Will do."

And that was that? 'Will do?' How lame!

Not bad for a first conversation. At least you know she sounds as sweet as she looks. And now you have something to do besides moon over a woman on surveillance videos. Get cutting!

Chapter 4
Hats off!

News item: Winter Carnival for Mesa Verde Elementary School is at 6:30 PM Friday. Parents are encouraged to bring their children and siblings to the fun-filled evening with games, presents, and a surprise visit by Santa Claus!

***

Now, how in the heck can they have a 'surprise' visit from Santa Claus if they just announced it on the school's web page, on bulletin boards all over this end of town, and even in the newspaper! These idiots are making it too easy for me. I'll just drop in and pretend I'm looking for someone. Well, I will be looking for Charlene and Chip, but they don't know that, so I guess I won't be lying. Keep a low profile, Arlie, no one will suspect anything. Don't lose your blending-in skills. You've only been away from the force for a week and you're rambling like an idiot.

"At least I'm not talking out loud. Shit. I just said that out loud. Why are you obsessing? You'd better get a new project, or at least plan more pillow covers, dude. You're coming apart at the seams."

Arlie's back suddenly twinged. "Crap!" he said and grabbed the kitchen counter. "Okay, it's all right to talk to yourself. Stop beating yourself up. You figured it out a long time ago, as soon as you get riled about something, muscles knot and *twang!* Just mosey on outside and let the sunshine warm up your muscles. Yeah, dude, you're livin' the easy life. You're still young, not bad looking, a decent savings account, not a care in the world..."

As soon as he hobbled down the two steps onto the small patio, his jaws clamped tight, his words shut off. Not that anyone was listening. The park was full of silver-haired and ball-capped seniors, but they all had their own agendas. It was Swap Meet Saturday and everyone—or so it seemed—was at the outdoor market, sampling exotic cuisines, scented candles, or hawking collectibles. Besides, the roar of cars and trucks traveling up and down Apache Boulevard drowned out even intentional conversations.

"Are you okay, Arlie?" Dave asked.

"Oh, hi, Dave. Ugh, I don't know. Sometimes I have back issues. It flares up every once in a while. I just need to relax until it quits spazzing."

"Well, I'm just next door if you need anything..." Arlie's

portly neighbor to the south stopped in mid-comment, turned around, and called out, "Davey, come over here and help this man unfold his chair."

"Yes, sir," the young boy answered. The screen door slammed on Grandpa's trailer door as he bounced out and rushed to Arlie's side. "Let me help, sir. These chairs can pinch your fingers if you're not careful. See?"

The blonde boy held up his bandaged middle finger, then blushed. "Oops. I didn't mean to show it to you that way."

Arlie laughed at inadvertently being flipped off, then groaned at the pain laughing caused. He closed his eyes, willing his lower back to relax. "No offense taken. Do you live here, too?" he asked. "I've never seen you around."

"No, sir. I'm just visiting Grandpa. He said he's going to help me set up for the Winter Carnival at school on Friday. You can come, too, if you'd like. They said that Santa's going to be there."

Arlie leaned against the railing to the steps instead of sitting down. "Davey, would you do me a favor? On the counter is a bottle of pills and my water bottle. Would you bring them to me, please?"

"Yes, sir!" the boy said, then popped up the stairs, happy

to be of assistance.

"I've never seen a child so eager to help," Arlie said, making conversation. *This just might be the in I need at the school.*

"Here you are, sir. Do you need anything else?"

Arlie took the bottle, poured out four Ibuprofen, then gave it back. "Here, I'll trade you for the water. Could you put this back on the counter for me, please?"

"Yes, sir."

"Davey, why don't you let us adults talk for a bit. Here's my mailbox key. Go ahead and check the mail and put it on the table. I'll be back in a few minutes."

"Yes, sir," he said, then raced to the other end of the trailer park.

"How's your back now, Arlie. You look a little better."

Arlie set his water bottle on the steps, then gently eased himself into the chair. "Tension makes it flare up." He laughed, then groaned. "But I guess it's really caused by anger. I swear, every time I get pissed off about something, it twinges. I guess it's negative bio-feedback or something."

Don't let anyone know of your limitations. And emotional stress really is a trigger.

"So, do you need any help setting up for the carnival?" Arlie asked. "I may seem like a semi-invalid now, but it's better already."

"Actually, Arlie, you'd be getting me out of a bind if you did. You see, I had already volunteered to help, then the Santa they hired had to back out, so I told them I'd be his replacement. That left them one helper short." Dave patted his ample belly. "Me? Santa Claus? Imagine that! No padding required, just the costume, fake beard and a wig. They're always short of volunteers at the school. I'll just call and tell them that you're coming. I guess I'll have to fib to Davey and tell him I can't go help. I'm not sure if he believes in Santa still or not. I think he *wants* to believe but knows better. I guess he'll either recognize me or not."

"That's great that you help out. I'm waiting to hear about a job at Sprawl-Mart. I should know later today, tomorrow at the latest. I'll let them know I won't be able to work this Friday evening. Oh, and I already know where the school is."

"Just be there by 5:30. I think all you have to do is set up tables and chairs and such."

Davey popped in and waited for a break in the conversation. "There was nothing in the mailbox, Grandpa.

Can we make some popcorn?"

Dave patted his grandson on the shoulder. "That sounds like a great idea." He turned to Arlie, "I just remembered I have something that might help your back. I took an old idea and kicked it up about ten notches. I think I'll start selling them out at the swap meet if I can find a good source of old stereo magnets. I buy those cheap back braces, pull out the rinky dink magnets they use, then put in a couple heavy duty stereo magnets. You know—or maybe you don't—the ones they used in monster speakers back in the 70s? Works for me. Indulge an old man and see if it works. I'll send one over with Davey. You're too young to be hobbling around like an old man. Oh, if you need anything, just call out. I may be old, but my hearing's still keen."

Arlie kicked back in the webbed chair, warmth, contentment, and a double-dose of anti-inflammatory easing the tension in his back. "I'll try anything at this point. Enjoy your grandson. He's a keeper."

Yeah, he's a keeper. You may be lousy at relationships, but at least you helped make a child. Even if the boy may never know who you are, he wouldn't be alive if it weren't for you.

Why did you pull such a thoughtless prank? Going to a sperm bank just so you could pay off Jake early and get him to shut up?

It may have been thoughtless, but the 'donation' allowed Charlene to have a child. Never once in all those peeks into her life via surveillance cameras did she look like she didn't want Chip. You gave her a gift. She just doesn't know it was you who did the giving.

***

Friday, 6:30 PM

Mesa Verde Multi-Purpose Room

"Take off that hat! You know better than to wear a hat inside!"

The angry dark-haired mother snatched the ball cap off the boy's head. "And who said you could cut your hair!" She gasped and stood back in shock. "But…but…you're not Carlos!"

Chip took his hat out of the stunned woman's hand. "No, ma'am, I'm not. He's over there," pointing to the other red-haired boy who was waiting in line to see Santa.

Charlene walked up to her son and the mother of the new boy in school. "Hi, I'm Charlene. We've never met, but I've heard all about the 'twin' who just joined my son's class. Chip and Carlos really do look a lot alike." Charlene looked at the dark-haired, dark-eyed woman and said, "He must take after his father," then winced as she realized that the boy could be adopted.

"No. He does not look like his father and that is why we are separated," the woman replied sharply, then sighed. "I'm sorry. It is a very sore spot for me. I love my son, but his father does not. He has dark hair like mine. Carlos and his red hair was a…surprise."

Charlene could tell the woman was tormented and embarrassed about revealing her marital status to a woman who didn't even know her name. "Let's get some of that punch before it's gone. At least we don't have to worry about it being spiked. I think these kids are too young to even think about it."

"I wish it was spiked. I could use a drink right now." The woman shook her head and groaned. "Excuse me. I should not have said that. Let's start over. Hello, my name is Rosa. I'm new to this area. I used to live in Alaska, but moved to Costa Rica before my son was born. We just moved back to the USA. I'd love to go back to Anchorage, but not in the winter. I decided to give Arizona a try. It's drier than Costa Rica, but," she shut her eyes and smiled, "it is nice and warm during the days. I think I'll stay here forever!"

Arlie watched as the two women chatted. He caught bits and pieces of their conversation: 'drink right now,' Alaska, and Costa Rica. He followed their gaze. Shit! Two of them! The two boys looked like twins! Their noses were different, but other than their haircuts, they were practically identical. Had the other mother gone to Costa Rica and had a son there? That would explain everything. Hmm. Neither woman had a drink in her hand. It was time for Sir Galahad to come to the rescue.

"Good evening, ladies. I noticed you didn't have a drink yet. Here," he handed each of them a small paper cup of sherbet-laced fruit punch, "compliments of the friends and family of the students of Mesa Verde Elementary."

The women accepted their drinks with polite thank yous, then turned away.

Drat! Don't let this opportunity slip away!

"I'm new to this area, ladies. Maybe you could help me. I thought my nephew went to this school. Maybe you know him? He'd be in either first grade or kindergarten. His name is Jake Spinelli, Jr."

Charlene shook her head, "No, never heard of him. I don't think he's in kindergarten, though. They have two classes here, and I help both teachers with reading and crafts once a week. I've never heard that name in either one of them, though."

Arlie looked to Rosa. She was as white as new fallen snow. She swallowed hard to compose herself and answered. "I'm new here, too. I don't know any of the other students. Other than enrolling my son here on Monday, this is the first time I've been to this school."

"Ah," Arlie said casually, his inner fox sated at the discovery of the missing mother, "then he must be in first grade." He lifted his empty cup in salute. "Time for a refill. Enjoy the carnival," then turned away, his broad grin beaming.

"Excuse me, sir. Are one of these children yours?" the woman with the name tag 'Mrs. Sheffield' asked.

Arlie looked around, wondering why the principal of the school would have stopped him. Ah, predators…

"Oh, Mrs. Sheffield! I'm Arlie Biggar. Davey's grandfather," he bent closer to her and whispered, "You know, Santa

Claus?" He resumed his speaking tone, "Big Dave asked me to come give you a hand. I'm sorry, but I don't know the procedure. Should I have checked in with the office first?"

Mrs. Sheffield bit back a grin of embarrassment. "Only during school hours. This event was open to the public. It's just we have a new student whose mother said there were some custody issues." She looked at Arlie again. "You may have the same coloring as her son, but she said the father was big—very big—and had black hair with eyes almost the same color. I'm sorry to have detained you. Thank you for helping us with the event."

"You do need me to hang around—or maybe come back later—to help clean up, correct?"

"Oh, yes, I'd appreciate that so much. Most of the parents who come early to help set up have to take their children home afterwards and settle them down after all the excitement. Davey was so proud that his grandpa's neighbor offered to help us. He's such a dear boy."

"Yes, he is. Great manners are easy to teach, but unfortunately, not many parents take the time."

Since when did you become an expert on parenting? Shut up and make yourself scarce until it's time to clean up. You have research to do! Crap! What's the boy's last name now?

"Excuse me, I think I left my hat in the kindergarten classroom. Could you let me in?"

"Certainly. Come this way."

That was slick. Now she's even leading you to the classroom. She didn't even question why you'd even been in there."

"Go ahead and see if you can find it. I need to get back to the event. The door will automatically lock behind you. Thanks again for helping."

Cool! All the desks have first and last names on them. Look at that, little dotted lines so they know how big to make each letter. Geez, we did that when I was a kid, too. I guess teaching kids how to write hasn't changed, just how to do math.

Voila! Carlos Smith. Crap! That means Mom is using an alias and isn't very clever. Yeah, well it must run deep if the principal knows about it. Then again, according to statistics, about half these kids are—or will be—from divorced or single parent families.

Arlie ran his hand over Chip's name tag, then looked two desks away at Carlos's. Not twins, but definitely brothers. Get back to the party and see what else you can find, Detective Biggar.

***

"Thanks for letting me look, Mrs. Sheffield. I feel like such a dolt. I didn't wear the hat inside—I left it in the car. I'll make myself useful while we're waiting for this thing to wind down and clean up some of these paper plates and cups."

"You're such a doll, Arlie. One of the other mothers said you were looking for your nephew. I think she said Jake something-or-other. We don't have any kindergarteners or first-graders named Jake this year."

Arlie frowned in feigned concentration. "I was sure this was the school, but I guess I was wrong. I'll call my brother-in-law and ask him which school. Oh, well."

"I guess that's easy to do. The Mesa School District is the largest in the nation. Now, I'd better get back to mixing with the parents," she said, and waved good-bye.

Well, you were just now mixing with one of the parents. You just didn't know it.

Chapter 5
Pizza and wine

Trivia item: DNA tests are so efficient today that a person's genetic heritage can be obtained by a small amount of saliva. Is there a question about a person's maternity or paternity? Home kits are available for around $100 to test for either. DNA tests can also identify individuals. The FBI's CODIS (Combined DNA Index System) is a separate database for criminals or those arrested in association with a crime but is not available to the general public.

***

"Here, let me take those empties from you," Arlie said, taking the paper cups from Rosa and Charlene. "I'm sort of the volunteer janitor tonight. Thanks for coming!" he said with genuine enthusiasm.

Rosa's on the right, Charlene's on the left… He gently folded the paper cups and shoved them in his pants pocket. Looks like they passed on seconds for punch and have been drinking water instead. Great! DNA testing for two, coming up!

***

Arlie got back to his rented home and emptied his pockets

onto the counter. "R for Rosa on the right and L for Charlene on the left. He grabbed a pen and marked the cups R and C, then looked at his watch. "Dang. It's six o'clock in Anchorage. Maybe Abby's working late. Worth a try."

"Arlie? Is this Arlie?" she asked.

"I should have known you'd remember my number, Abby. What's going on?"

"Same ol', same ol' for me, but it must not be for you or you wouldn't be calling me. I hear you're in Phoenix."

"Close. I'm in Mesa. Hey, I got some paper cups I need DNA tested. Can I Express Mail them to you and see what you can find against CODIS? I think one of these is from a bad pajama mama. If she is, the FBI is sure to have a profile on her."

"Yeah, I think I can do it for you. Put them in separate baggies right away so they don't contaminate each other or dry out. I'm good at what I do, but I can't test what isn't there."

"Thanks, gal. I owe you a big wet one."

"Ew! I'd rather have a big wet one from your girlfriend. Do you have one yet?"

"Abby, you know I don't have time for relationships..."

"Arlie, that line worked when you were putting in twenty-five hours a day, eight days a week. You're semi-retired now from what I hear."

"Nah. I think I'm going back to work here in a few days."

"For the Mesa PD?"

"Nope, and I hope you're sitting down for this. I'll be working for Sprawl-Mart. Looks like I'm going to be one of Santa's helpers, putting bicycles together."

Abby laughed so hard, she started coughing. "You, putting together bicycles? Next thing you'll be saying is that you're going to be playing Santa on your days off."

"No, but I do live next door to Santa." He took a deep breath and asked, "Would you keep this on the down low and off any official records?"

Abby laughed. "I guess this really is top secret stuff. You've never asked me to do that before, Mr. Play-by-the-rules."

"Well, this is personal."

"You got it, A. I'll get the answers to you within 24 hours of receiving your samples. Just don't get sunburned out there. And for goodness sake, get a girlfriend!"

"Abby..."

"Okay. At least get laid."

***

Chip tapped on his mother's elbow to get her attention. "Mom, can we go get pizza after this is done? I'm still hungry."

"Yeah, I want pizza, too," Carlos said. "We never go anywhere anymore."

Rosa looked down at her son. "We came here tonight, didn't we?"

"Yeah, well…"

"But you're right. Pizza sounds good," Rosa said. "Charlene, would you like to join us for a late dinner? There's no school for the boys tomorrow."

"I, um…"

Rosa could tell that money was an issue, so quickly squelched that excuse. "My treat tonight. I've been wanting a glass of wine for hours…"

"If you'd like, I can drive and you can have your wine," Charlene said.

"That would be fantastic. Boys, go get those little gifts they gave you and your jackets. We're going to have an after-party party!"

"Why don't I follow you to your house so we can drop off your car? This way I'll know where you live if you have too much to drink," Charlene said, and laughed.

Rosa frowned, then realized her new friend had made a joke. Charlene couldn't possibly know that she'd had that problem on more than one occasion. She laughed belatedly and said. "I'm sorry, Charlene. I misunderstood you at first. Yes, I'm just a few blocks away. It isn't much because it's just a rental, but it's home for now."

Rosa stopped in her driveway but didn't get out right away. When she did, she came to Charlene's side of the car, her face red with anger. "I'm sorry I'm holding everyone up. I told my son not to play with the garage door opener. Now he's left it the house and I can't put the car inside. I don't have my house key either, but don't worry. I have keypad access. Let's just go now so we can get dinner for the boys. I'll leave the car outside while we're gone. Oh, and I'll write down the security code for you in case I forget it after my wine," she said, then giggled.

"Come on Carlos," she called. "You get to ride in the back with Chip."

If Alonzo hadn't found her car by now, he never would.

Removing the Lo-jack before it left the port in Costa Rica was a great idea but attaching the device to a vintage Jeep and sending it by slow boat to Madrid was pure genius. If she had smashed it, he would have known that she was on to him. She had at least another week to go before that ship reached Spain. He may have married her for her boobs, but she had brains, too.

***

"Mama, Mama, can I get some coins for the machine? I want to show Chip how I can grab the toys with the claw. He said he doesn't think I can do it."

Rosa reached into her purse and fumbled around until she pulled out a twenty-dollar bill. "Go get some change and give half of it to Chip. Maybe you can show him some of your secret moves."

Charlene's eyes widened at the generosity. By the looks of the huge two-story house that Rosa considered modest and the Maserati she drove, she must have lots of money. Maybe being friends with someone whose background was so different wasn't a good idea. She'd never be able to keep up with the clothes and gifts she was sure to give her son. Shoot! Rosa's house was bigger than her four-plex!

"Rosa, you don't need to give my son money. I never let him play those games. They're worse than gambling. Only the house wins."

"It's okay. It's his father's money. The old man has more than he needs anyway. Besides, now the boys will be busy for a while and I can enjoy my wine." She drained the glass in one long, slow drink, appreciation showing in her smile and soft sigh when she was done.

"I haven't had a drink in three weeks. Life has been a bit tense for me lately."

"May I take your order, please?" the young waitress asked.

"I don't know about Carlos, but Chip likes plain cheese pizza."

Rosa giggled, then stifled a hiccup. "So does Carlos. What kind do you want?"

Charlene shrugged her shoulder. "Whatever you're getting is fine by me."

Rosa lifted her empty wine glass to the waitress. "I'll have another rosé, please. How about an extra-large cheese pizza and an extra-large meaty one? The more meat, the better for me!" she said and giggled, then put her hand up to cover another hiccup.

Charlene started to protest about the amount of food she was ordering, then realized that Rosa was probably anticipating having leftovers to take home. Well, whether the woman had more money than she did or not, at least she was generous and considerate of others' feelings.

"Excuse me," Rosa said after her third glass of wine. She reached into her purse and pulled out another twenty-dollar bill. "I have to use the restroom. If the boys come back, give them money for more change. It's celebration time! Independence Day for me, all over again!"

Rosa toddled to the ladies room, grabbing onto the backs of the booths on her way, then made a detour to the bar on her way back. Carlos was distracted and she had someone to look after him if he got tired of playing 'the claw.' Maybe she could pawn him off on Charlene for the night. The two boys got along great. He'd never had a best friend before. His 'father' and all those private tutors and body guards ensured that. He was long overdue for companionship from someone his own age.

***

He really hadn't followed the women after they left the

school, but pizza did sound good. There were three pizza restaurants in the area and only two of them were family friendly. Maybe it was luck, but he spotted Charlene's white Subaru Outback at the first one. He sat in his lemon-yellow Beetle in the parking lot, dialed the restaurant, and ordered his favorite pizza.

After five minutes of physical discomfort from sitting still— and emotional angst from not being able to see the boys who were just on the other side of the beige-stucco facade, he decided to wait inside. Sitting on a bar stool was much more comfortable, allowing his back to stretch out, and if there were security cameras inside, he could watch the boys from anywhere on his smartphone, no matter where everyone sat.

"Hi, I called in a pizza for Arlie. I'm probably early..."

"Oh, shoot!" the silver-haired hostess said. "I forgot to give the guys in back the order. It was half Hawaiian, half pepperoni and sausage, right?"

Arlie nodded, then looked over. *He wouldn't have to eye-in-the-sky spy on his sons and their mothers. The boys were at the Mega Claw game, trying for stuffed action figures and trinkets, and Charlene was sitting two tables away.* "Oh, yeah," he said to the hostess, back to reality. "Right. It's okay. Don't worry about it. I'll wait. I'm not in a hurry."

"Can I get you something to drink while you wait? On the house, of course."

"Just give me a Sprite or whatever. No ice, please."

The hostess turned to get the ginger-haired man his drink, then saw the brunette beauty give him the once-over. Years of experience wasn't needed to see that this gal was on the prowl. She had come in with another woman—her designated driver—but it looked like she wanted to go home with this good-looking guy. She didn't blame her. If she was twenty years younger and not married, she'd go after him, too. Time for a little match-making.

"Arlie, right?" the hostess asked.

He nodded in reply, keeping his face stoic, then realized he had given his name when he ordered the pizza, and smiled.

"Here, I put your drink in a wine glass. It looks like someone is interested in you," she said, glancing sideways to the young Natalie Wood look-alike. "It might look a little better if you had a real drink in your hand, but this will work just as well."

Rosa strolled over, her eyes fixed on him. "Oh, hi," she

said, then stumbled and fell into his arms.

Arlie caught her limp and looped body. "Are you all right?"

She looked up at him, comfortable in his hold, not even trying to stand up or move away. "I will be if you tell me your name. I don't like the idea of being in someone's arms if I don't know his name." She grinned, then hiccupped and covered her mouth. "Oh, excuse me!"

Arlie helped her onto the stool next to his. "All right. Hi, I'm Arlie. I guess we already have something in common: we're both new to Mesa. I saw you briefly at the school. Oh, and since you've been in my arms," he said, giving her what he hoped was a sexy bachelor smile, "How about letting me know *your* name?"

"I'm Rosa De Lu..." Rosa paused to think, then started again. "I'm Rosa Smith."

Arlie couldn't help but chuckle, not that she noticed. Her forehead was now nestled in his shoulder and she was sighing into his tee shirt.

"You smell good," she said. "I haven't been this close to a man in a long, long time."

"Are you all right, Rosa," Charlene asked, her hand on Rosa's back. "You went to the restroom and never came back."

Rosa turned her face toward Charlene but left the top of her head in Arlie's shoulder. "I sure am!"

Arlie straightened up and gently removed Rosa from his body. He mouthed, 'I think she's had too much to drink,' to Charlene, then said aloud, "Hi, I'm Arlie. I met you two briefly at the school tonight. Looks like you four are out for a little Friday night fun. I just dropped in for take-out pizza. I'll let you ladies get back to your table."

"Are you sure you don't want to join us?" Rosa asked, her bottom lip stuck out in an exaggerated pout.

"No, thanks. It looks like you're having a private party."

"If you take me to your place, we can have a private party."

"Rosa!" Charlene hissed. "What are you going to do with Carlos?"

"He can spend the night with you, can't he?" she asked with a grin, then wiped under her nose and whispered, 'Please.'

"I'm sorry," Arlie said, looking at Rosa, then catching Charlene's eye. "I have some work to do tonight. Maybe some other time."

"Mama, Mama! Look what we won!" Carlos said, tugging on his mother's arm, an armload of stuffed animals clutched close to his chest. "I showed Chip how to win at the claw and now he's good at it, too!"

Rosa pulled away from Arlie, sniffed back the embarrassment of begging for a date, then turned to Carlos. "That's wonderful, son. I'm so glad you have a friend now."

"Mommy, can Carlos spend the night tonight?" Chip asked, "Please, please, pretty please?"

Arlie watched the interaction of the boys and their mothers, not needing to hide his smile of appreciating how sweet the young ones looked, vicariously sharing their excitement of winning games and discovering a new friendship.

"Let's go eat our pizza and figure it out afterwards," Charlene told the boys, herding both them and Rosa toward their table. "It should be cool enough to eat by now." She turned back and said, "Nice meeting you, Arlie. Enjoy your pizza. It's the best in the valley."

"You, too," he said, then realized she hadn't introduced herself and he hadn't asked.

Oh, well. Another day, maybe. He chuckled softly. No,

another day, for sure!

"Arlie, your pizza's ready," the hostess said, breaking his reverie. "I guess they overheard me take the order so I sorta didn't screw up. Sorry if I messed up, trying to set you up with her. I've never seen her in here before and she, well, she looked kinda lonely."

"And I did, too?" Arlie asked, then laughed. "Nah, don't worry about it. I met the ladies and their sons earlier tonight."

"*Their* sons? I thought they were twins!"

"They sure look alike, that's for sure." Arlie set down a twenty. "Here, keep the change. I not only have dinner but won't have to worry about breakfast or lunch tomorrow, either."

Chapter 6
Secret Brothers

News item: Depending on how many facial recognition features are used and who does the calculating, the chance of having a doppelganger ranges from one in 74,000 to one in one trillion!

***

"Uh oh. Charlene, did I pull into the driveway or did I back in?"

"I'm pretty sure you pulled in forwards. Does someone else have a key to your car?" Charlene answered as they drove up to the house.

"Yes, my soon-to-be ex does, but I didn't think he knew where I lived. Would you wait out here while I go inside and look around?"

"Sure, no problem. If you want, I'll call the cops first if you think there might be trouble."

"No, I don't think he's that stupid. Carlos, wait here with Charlene and Chip. I'll be right back."

Rosa sniffed the air as she approached the front door. She may be half-smashed, but wherever Alonzo and Luca went, their special blend of eau pour homme lingered. Nope, no stink. She pushed the key pad code with the tip of her fingernail, then pressed the handle down using the hem of her blouse as a barrier to cover it. She didn't trust them not to put transdermal poison on either one of them. She'd have to remember to douse them with disinfectant spray cleanser in the morning.

It didn't appear anything had been moved. She checked the interior doors. Nope, her tattletale bits of dental floss above the closed interior doors were still in place. She grabbed them and quickly tossed them in the garbage, sniffing the air the whole time.

"Is everything all right?" Charlene asked, standing outside the front door threshold. "You were taking a while and I was afraid..."

"No, no. Everything's fine. I guess I'm a bit paranoid." She stood tall and took a deep calming breath, "And a little drunk. Thanks for having my back."

"The boys want to know if Carlos can spend the night. You don't have to worry about getting any pajamas for him—Chip has plenty—and I always keep a new toothbrush on hand. It's fine with me if you think you'll be okay..."

"It might be better if he went with you. I don't think there's a problem, but I'm not much fun to be around. I have a good book to read, so I'm set. Thanks. I appreciate all you've done for me. I usually don't drink because I have a problem stopping at one. This separation has really been tough on me." She shook her head, trying to erase all the horrors she'd gone through in the last three weeks. "I don't have any friends around here. Shoot, who am I fooling? I haven't made a new friend, or reconnected with an old friend, since before Carlos was born. My husband was *very* controlling."

"Well, here's my phone number." Charlene reached in her coat pocket and found an old receipt and a pen. She scribbled her name and number on the back of it. "Call me if you ever need anything. And if life gets tough, Carlos can stay with us for as long as you need."

Rosa took the paper and let out a huge sigh of relief. "You have no idea how much that means to me. All the money in the world isn't as precious as a friend I can count on. Now, on the flipside, if you need anything, you let *me* know." She put her hand out, pointing to the entertainment center loaded with a huge curved screen TV, a Blu-ray player, and assorted speakers on the walls. "As you can see, I have money and

I'm not afraid to spend it."

Charlene stepped closer and wrapped her arms around Rosa's shoulders. "Now, don't hesitate to call me if you need anything. Or call 911 if you think he's hanging around or... Well, just don't take any chances, all right?"

"Yes, Mommy," Rosa said and laughed. "I'll be fine."

***

After one more reading of The Night Before Christmas, Charlene tucked both boys into Chip's twin bed. Carlos had fallen asleep half-way through the second time, but Chip had begged, 'Just one more time...'

"Mommy, before I go to sleep, can I ask you something?"

"Of course, dear."

"Well, when Carlos and I were playing the claw game, he told me some stuff. He really didn't tell me *not* to tell you, but he did say it was a secret. Is it okay if I tell you since you're my mom?"

"Honey, anytime anyone tells you something is a secret and you think it's important, yes, please tell me. I won't let on that you told me. So, go ahead. I don't think he'll hear you. He's sound asleep."

"Well, he said he and his mom had to leave their old home

51

in Coca Cola because his dad wanted to kill them."

"Oh, my. That is important. Did he say anything else?"

"Yeah, he said his dad's going to be really mad if he and his uncle ever do catch up to him and his mom because she took a whole bunch of money. But she said it was all right because she was his wife and half of everything he had was hers anyway. She was real smart and had her car shipped to America before they left so it'd be here when they got here. His father wanted her Macaroni car, too, but Carlos said that since his dad gave it to his mom for a birthday gift, she said it was really all hers."

Charlene didn't bother correcting Chip on Costa Rica and Maserati, but now it was beginning to make sense. Sort of. Why would a man want to kill his own son?

"Did Carlos tell you why his father wanted to kill him?"

"Yeah. He said his dad did some kind of test—an ABC or CDE or something like that test—and it said that he wasn't really his dad. His dad said that Carlos was a buzzard. Then his mom got real mad and started yelling and… Then Carlos started to cry and said he didn't want to talk about it anymore."

So, Rosa's husband did a DNA test and found out he

wasn't the father and called the boy a bastard. Shoot, I'd get mad and start yelling, too!

"He said his mom says they'll be all right, though, because they have all that money. He said she keeps it in a big bag of dog food." Chip giggled. "That's kinda funny because they don't have a dog. He says he wants one, but she keeps telling him later..."

Charlene watched as her son's eyes blinked, then stayed shut. He'd had a big evening. She looked up at the Minions clock on the wall. Ten o'clock. He hadn't stayed up this late since he was a baby.

***

"Mom, since it's Saturday and you don't have to work, can we go to the mall and see Santa? I want to ask him for something," Chip said, then picked up his bowl and slurped the last of the milk from his cereal.

Brrrng, brrng, brrng.

"Hello. Oh, hi, Rosa. Yes, they did great. They're just finishing up their cereal. I think they both want to go to the mall and see Santa, right, boys?"

"Santa, Santa, Santa," the boys cheered, jumping up and down, then hugging each other. "Santa, Santa, Santa."

"Settle down, you two, so I can hear Rosa." Charlene's face fell at the news, then she pasted on a fake smile for the boy's sake. "I'll go ahead and take them and give you a call when I get back. What's your number? It says unknown caller on my caller ID."

Charlene grabbed the dry erase marker off the top of the refrigerator and scribbled on the freezer. "Okay. Got it. Take whatever time you need. If you don't get back until late, he can spend the night again. I don't have to go back to work until Monday just after I drop off Chip at daycare. All right. Take care of yourself. Bye, now."

Charlene ignored the twittering of the boys and tapped on her phone, entering Rosa's phone number. "Just a minute. Hold still you two or we won't be going anywhere."

The boys folded their arms, then looked at each other and giggled when they realized that they had both made the same gesture.

Just in case, I'll give her an alias. Not that anyone's going to get into my phone. Better make sure it's one I'll remember. She looked over at Carlos. *She looks like a Carla to me. Carlos and Carla. That's an easy one.*

"Okay, boys. Put your dishes in the dishwasher, then

brush your teeth. Chip, there's a new toothbrush in the top drawer. That one now belongs to Carlos."

"Is he going to live here now, Mom?"

"Nooo… His mother has a few errands to run and asked if he could spend time with you. I didn't ask you because…"

"Because you knew I'd say yes, huh?"

"No, because I didn't think I needed to ask you an easy question. Now, snap to it, guys. Santa's waiting!"

***

There were already twenty people in front of the boys at Santa's Workshop at the mall. 'Santa arrives at 10:00. Get a picture with Santa for only $10.' Charlene groaned. Another heartbreaking moment of having to say no.

"What does that say, Charlene?" Carlos asked.

"It says Santa will be here in ten minutes. That seems like a long time, but look how many people are behind us. They have to wait a lot longer than we do."

The boys turned around and saw children and parents of all ages, shapes, and sizes queuing up. "At least we get to see him before Christmas. I'm going to ask him for a Stingray bicycle," Chip said to Carlos.

"I already got one. I'm going to ask him for a brother! Mom

said she can't have any more, but I still want a brother!"

Chip whispered in Carlos's ear, "Mom said I can't have a baby brother or baby sister or nothing, not even a dog. I kinda want a dad, too. Actually, I'd rather have a dad than anything, but mom said that ain't gonna happen."

Carlos put his hand to Chip's head and whispered, "My mom said all she wants for Christmas is to get rid of my dad. I guess it should make me sad, but he never did anything with me. He wouldn't even eat dinner with us!"

"What are you two whispering about? Oh, if it's a secret that won't get anyone in trouble, you don't have to tell me."

"Nah," Chip said. "We're just telling each other what we want from Santa. I can't tell you, just Santa, 'cause I know we don't have a lot of money."

"We're next!" Carlos said.

"You can go ahead of me," Chip offered, "Because you're new around here so that kinda makes you younger."

Carlos frowned at almost being called a baby, then smiled as he realized that that meant he got to tell Santa what he wanted first.

"Go ahead and sit on Santa's lap there while I take your picture," the teenager dressed in green tights and a mini skirt elf costume said.

"Oh, no," Charlene said. "We're not getting the pictures. The boys just wanted to tell Santa what they want. There's no charge for that, I hope!"

"Oh, no charge. I'll snap the picture and if you don't want it, you don't have to keep it. They're digital, not Polaroid, so there's no cost involved until it's printed out."

Charlene grimaced at her Grinch attitude, then relaxed as the boys went up one after the other to share their secret wishes with the well-costumed Santa.

"How about if I take a picture with the twins together?" the elf-lady asked.

"Oh, no, they're not twins, just friends, but go ahead. Like you said, it won't cost until it's printed."

"Wow! That's awesome! They really do look alike except for the haircuts. How much for this?" Charlene asked as she rummaged through her purse.

"It's ten bucks a picture, so that's twenty bucks if you want the other mother to have a copy."

"Oh, yeah…"

"I got this, Charlene," Carlos said, and pulled a twenty-dollar bill out of this pocket. "Mom said that this was for emergencies or if it was something I really, really wanted. Not just wanted today kinda wanted like a candy bar, but something I'd want to have when I was her age. I think she'd want me to use my money for this."

"You're right. I never thought about it like that. Here's ten dollars for my copy…"

"My treat," Carlos said. "You can get it next time."

"All right," Charlene said. "You sounded just like your mother when you said that."

"Really? Thanks! Can we go to the toy store and just look around?"

"Ooh! Ooh!" Chip said, holding on to Carlos's arm. "And then can we go to the pet store? I wanna look at the puppies!"

Chapter 7
Faster than a 747

Random Fact: It is approximately 4,000 miles from Mesa, Arizona to Anchorage, Alaska via the Al-Can Highway. It would take 5-7 days to drive that distance, 11 months to walk it, or 5 hours to fly it non-stop in a 747, the first two estimates dependent upon the traveler's need for sleep and the weather conditions.

***

"Good morning, sweetie."

"Arlie? What in the heck are you doing calling me on a Saturday morning? I thought I told you to get a life," Abby said, rolling over to look at the time. "Shit! It's only six o'clock!"

"No, you told me to get laid, but regardless, I just wanted to give you a heads up. I sent that *special handling* package to you on Alaska Airlines. It should have come in at 1:30 this morning."

"Wait. What? When did you ship it?"

"I took it down at ten last night... Oh, crap. Let me look. Dang, Abby, I'm sorry. It comes in this afternoon at 1:30. It couldn't make it there in under five hours, even if there was a

59

direct flight in the winter. Sorry again. Go back to bed."

"I am in bed, bozo, but I'll go back to sleep."

***

Arlie looked around his micro home, realized there was nothing to do but fret and fuss and fantasize, so grabbed the keys to the little VW bug he'd bought off CraigsList. Time for a cup of fancy coffee.

"How'd it go last night, Arlie?" Dave called out. "I saw you getting acquainted with a few young ladies."

"And the principal." Arlie chuckled. "Yeah, I never thought I'd spend a Friday night helping out a bunch of little kids and their parents. They're a whole different group of folks from what I'm used to. Oh, and that high fidelity back brace works great." Arlie pulled up his shirt and showed off the black nylon and Velcro modified cummerbund. "So, where's the best place to get a *macchiato*?"

"Well, I don't know if it's the best place, but if you want a change of scenery from the old folks on this end of town, you might want to head west. Take your pick of the super malls. They'll all have little shops in their food courts. Us old farts hang out at the swap meets and restaurants, but the under-40 set is usually at the mall. They got theaters in there, too, if you're looking for a bigger screen than what you have in that little Hobbit home of yours."

"I don't have a TV—just a smartphone and YouTube," Arlie said and chuckled. "But you're right. I need to get out and move around." Arlie reached one arm over his head. "I feel great this morning, even if I did lug around a dozen tables and three times that many folding chairs last night. Must be all those youthful 'hormones' in the air."

Dave tipped his neck side to side, loosening his tight Santa Claus muscles. "You didn't spend the evening with sixty squiggly, giggly kids on your lap, all of them wanting more than the last one. I did what I could to make them happy without making a direct promise. I held the line for about half of them, though. I told them I couldn't guarantee they'd get a little brother or sister or a puppy for Christmas. That was up to their folks."

Dave rolled his shoulder, still uncomfortable, then frowned. "Davey's spending the day with his father. I miss the boy already. Too bad his folks split up, but at least they're not divorced and both are civil to each other. I have to keep telling Davey that it wasn't his fault, that his folks are just taking a time out."

Arlie shut his eyes and grimaced. Remember, you gave those women the chance to become mothers, gave them sons they wouldn't have otherwise. He breathed a sigh of self-dispensation, then turned to his one and only Arizonan friend.

"I think I need that coffee more than I care to admit. I'll take you up on your idea about the mall. The parking lot there can't be any more crowded than the restaurants on this end of town."

"What can I say, Arlie? You came to Arizona to start a life right at the heart of snowbird season. It's almost dead around here in the summer. The heat sucks, but the privacy and parking are fantastic."

***

"Stay in the right lane, stay in the right lane," Arlie chanted to himself. "Good grief! Could they make these streets any wider? Parking lots in Anchorage aren't as wide as these roads!"

Arlie pulled into the first entrance to the mall, then paled at the vast rolling area that seemed to cover miles. "How in the hell am I going to find my way around? Well, it's a good thing I don't have anything else to do today or tomorrow. I might as

62

well get used to the crowds now."

Out of habit, Arlie grabbed his cane from the back seat, then put it back. "Work smarter, not harder. Pull up a map of the layout of the mall, find out where the food court or coffee shops are, see if any of the stores spark your fancy, then park next to that entrance." Arlie used his smartphone to locate the food court, then tapped and swiped a few more times to get a live satellite feed of the parking lot. "Aha! Someone's pulling out right now." He drove to that side of the massive building and waited for the geriatric driver to back up his vintage baby blue Cadillac Seville.

"Finally," Arlie huffed when he was able to pull into the spot. "I guess these guys have all the time in the world…"

And you don't? Come on, stop being such a wuss. The exercise will do you good. Just think, you could be back in Alaska, negotiating icy sidewalks, scraping frozen windshields, and dodging urban moose and criminal bullets. Just get your coffee, take in a little eye candy, and eat up the day until Abby gets back with the DNA results.

***

"Wow!"

"Yeah, really," the old man standing next to Arlie said. "An indoor carousel. What will they think of next?"

"I saw it on the…the map on the other side of the building, but I thought it was the name of a store, not a real—pardon the expression—dog and pony show."

"Yeah, it brings in the kids. And of course, the kids are brought in by parents or older siblings who shop. Yes, the twinkling lights, calliope music, and carved critters are a big draw for the merchants. Here," the tall gray-haired man in the 'Old Farts Rule' tee shirt said, "I got some tokens for my grandkids, and then they bailed on me. I need to leave, so if you see any little ones around, would you do me a favor and give these to them? I really need to get back and watch the Cardinals lose. Or win. Either way," the man looked at his bare wrist, "Since my grandkids aren't with me today, it's beer-thirty!"

"Sure, no problem. Enjoy the game. And the suds."

Arlie pocketed the tokens. It would have been rude to refuse them, and who knew? Maybe he could brighten someone's day. What goes around comes around he mused as he began his stroll through the parade of store fronts selling everything from sneakers to sweatshirts to snow globes.

Well, I'll be… Pat's Bike Shop. Maybe I can get some pointers in case I do get that job as a bicycle assembly technician at Sprawl-Mart.

"Good morning, sir. May I help you?"

"Right now, I'm just looking. Can you tell me what to look for in a quality bike?"

"You can have the fanciest alloy frame and more gears than you have fingers and toes, but if you have a crappy crankshaft, you're sunk," the short dark-haired salesman said.

"Oh, I didn't know that. And, pardon my ignorance, but what is a crankshaft on a bicycle?" Arlie asked, checking over the mountain bike perched on a pedestal in the window display.

"That's what the pedals are attached to." The salesman pointed to it on the bike. "You know, what you push with your feet to engage the chain to the sprocket and gears."

"Actually, I haven't spent much time on a bicycle, at least since I was about yea high," Arlie said, holding his hand to three feet tall. "I never paid much attention, though; just pedaled until the chain fell off."

"That's what happens when you don't have the right

tension on the chain. Here, let me show you."

Arlie was deep into learning about chain tension and *derailleurs* when he heard a familiar voice.

"Mommy, Mommy, come look! They got Stingrays and lots of other bikes in here." Chip paused in awe, then said. "That's all they have in here! I think I'm in bike heaven…"

"Cool," Carlos said. "Look at all those different seats! I just got a bike a few weeks ago, but I want one of those long seats with the big bar in back. What's it called?"

"Man, you two can sure move fast! I thought you wanted to ride the carousel?" Charlene said, not even trying to hide her exasperation. "Oh, all right. We can look around in here. Remember, don't touch anything. We're just looking."

"Excuse me, sir," the salesman said to Arlie. "I think I got a live one."

I'd sure like to have her as a live one!

Arlie groaned at his random, visceral thought, then stepped back against the wall—almost, but not quite—wishing he was invisible. Too late. Charlene had seen him.

"What are you doing here? Are you stalking me?" she asked, her lips pursed as if she was ready to scold him for writing on the walls with a permanent marker.

He shrugged one shoulder and said, "Hey, I was here first," then allowed a smile to creep in at the serendipity of the moment. "Really. I was just checking out bikes, same as you and the boys. Are you sure *you* aren't stalking *me*?"

"Of course not!" She huffed, then realized how rude she had been. She shook her head and sighed out a lungful of frustration. "I'm sorry. I have a lot on my mind. The boys are all wound up about Christmas." Charlene looked around the store and took in all the shiny bikes. "I wish there really was a Santa Claus. Chip wants a Stingray bike so bad… That's all he's talked about since last summer."

"Here's an inexpensive one," Arlie said, and picked up the little plastic globe with a miniature Stingray bike inside. "At least you don't have to worry about the tires going flat or the chain coming off."

Charlene chuckled. "Thanks, I needed that. I came in the other entrance so they wouldn't see the carousel, but then there were posters all over the place for it…" she said and allowed a small groan to escape. "Maybe I can distract them and they'll forget about it."

"Good luck with that." Arlie's eyes lit up. "Speaking of luck…" He reached into his pocket and pulled out a fistful of tokens. "Would you believe I was given these by a gentleman I met just after I came in? We started talking about the 'dog and pony' show, then he said his grandchildren stood him up. He'd already bought these and asked if I could hand them out to some deserving kids. Do you think," he nodded to the two boys who were pawing the assorted handle grips, "that they're deserving?"

"Oh, yeah," she replied, then paused. "So, you didn't just buy these to entice some young mother to have lunch with you?"

His face fell as he realized it did look strange. "No!" he said, then grinned. "But now that you mention it, that might be a novel come on. Nah, I'm not looking for anyone. I'm up for a job as a bike mechanic. Or engineer or assembly person…whatever they call it. I was just hoping to get a few pointers from this guy here. Looks like he's got a customer hooked on that big fifteen-speed bike, though."

Arlie looked at the boys, then turned back to her. "So, do you think the boys are ready to ride the carousel?"

"I'm pretty sure that'll pull them away from these bikes."

Arlie held the tokens out. "Here."

Charlene opened her hand for them. Arlie put his hand

under hers in case any spilled over. A spark of cosmic electricity shot through him at her touch. "You know, I never did get your name..."

"I'm Charlene, and you're Charlie, right?"

"Close. Just drop the 'chuh'. My legal first name is Charles, but I go by Arlie."

"That's Chip's first name, too. When he was born, he didn't look like a Charles or Charlie. I thought of Chuck and Chaz, but Chip just seemed to fit. Charles was my father's name, so he's named after family."

Charlene put the tokens in her purse, then called the boys. "Didn't you two want to ride the carousel today before we left?"

"Ooh, ooh!" they chanted, then came to her side, clinging to her arm. "We can go?"

"Yes, it seems we've been gifted some tokens by this man here. Say thank you to Arlie."

"Thank you, Arlie," the boys chorused.

"Are you coming with us?" asked Carlos.

"No, no. I just came in to browse the shops and get a cup of coffee. Have a great rest of the morning, boys. And Mom."

"She's not your mom," Chip said. "She's my mom."

"You're right. Have a nice rest of the *day*, Charlene."

"You, too, Arlie."

A few more 'bye-byes' were said, and then they were gone, their absence like a plate of spaghetti licked clean. Empty. And he wanted more.

What got into you, dedicated detective and bachelor? Now that you don't have bad guys to chase down, you think you need a family to fill up your life?

Arlie stepped out into the promenade and looked around to orient himself to where the nearest coffee shop was, hoping the voices in his head would at least change subjects.

Of course, the closest coffee shop is near the carousel. Even if it wasn't, you'd wind up down there anyhow. You're smitten, dude. Just like a hormonal teenager, you won't be satisfied until you see her again. And again. And then you'll want to see her again.

Arlie gritted his teeth at his inner conflict, wishing he didn't have feelings for the young mother. Even if she wasn't the mother of his son, he'd be attracted to her. Even if she wasn't buxom with the prettiest legs he'd seen in years, he'd want to be close to her. Very close. Yes, what attracted him to her was her keen sense of right and wrong, the willingness to take on a huge law firm and fight, even when she knew that with time and money they would probably win. She came to Rosa's rescue when it looked like her new friend was going to spend the night with a stranger. He wouldn't take advantage of an inebriated woman, but Charlene didn't know that.

"May I have your order, please?"

Arlie realized he was already where he wanted to go and smiled at the bubbly blonde barista. He looked up at the menu. *Only four flavors and four styles? Where did these people learn coffee appreciation?*

"I'll have a large caramel macchiato, extra foam, please."

"That'll be $7.53, sir."

Arlie pulled out two fives. "I don't need any change. I'll just wait over here."

Charlie watched children run around the cordoned off area, bouncing up and down, asking moms or dads for more tokens. Why did they suddenly look charming?

"Here you go, sir. You can use the tables and stools around the corner, just before you get to the carousel. That's where the parents usually wait. Oh, and watch out. I think it might be a little too hot."

Arlie took the colorful paper cup of coffee and quickly changed hands. Even with the insulated sleeve, it was nearly too hot to handle. He definitely needed a flat surface to set it down on and soon.

"Are you stalking me again?" Charlene asked, then laughed.

"What? No, no... I didn't even see you. I knew you were coming to the carousel, but the barista made this macchiato so hot, I can't hold it, even with this phony paper sleeve on it."

"I'm just messing with you, Arlie. Yeah, I learned soon after moving here not to get anything but a drip coffee in this town. No one knows how to steam a decent cappuccino. Before I moved to Arizona, I lived in a little town called Eagle River. There were more coffee shops than gas stations, churches, and grocery stores combined. Really! In one little two block strip on the main drag, there were three of them. And all on the same side of the road. And that didn't include the grocery store or the gas station across the street that served it, too. The funny thing is, all three were always packed. Great coffee, awesome sandwiches and pastries...."

"Sounds heavenly," Arlie said, and grinned. He knew

exactly where she was talking about. He'd been in both the little independents cafés. "Salted caramel bars…"

"Yeah, those were my favorite, too. You can't get them around here, so I stopped looking. Long ago, in my former life where I had money, I bought a little cappuccino machine. It still works great, so I make myself a latte or mocha every morning before I go to work."

"Braggart," Arlie said without thinking. "Oh, I'm sorry. That was rude."

"Nah, you're just jealous because you paid over six bucks for that sugared mud. But hey, try it if it's cooled down enough. Maybe you got lucky and got a good one."

Arlie pulled the plastic lid off the cup and tried a sip, visualizing a tasty drink so even if it was nasty, she'd see him smile. "Here, try it and see what you think?"

Charlene sipped from the other edge of his cup and frowned. "Ew!"

Arlie leaned back and laughed, then put his hand to his mouth to try and stop. "I'm sorry. I shouldn't have done that. It's awful, I know. I may have to buy a cappuccino machine, too."

"Hey Mom, Arlie! Look at us!" the boys called out, riding

double on the carousel dragon.

Charlene and Arlie stood up to get a better look. "Be careful, boys," Charlene hollered.

"We are," they called back. "Thanks, Arlie!"

"Well, it looks like you found someone to share the tokens with," the man said as he walked up to stand next to Arlie.

"Hey, there. Yes, I did." Arlie shook the man's hand. "The boys said thanks to me, but it should have been to you."

Arlie did a double take at the man's Dallas Cowboys jersey. "I thought you had to go home and toast the Cardinals, whether they won or lost."

The old man laughed. "I was going to, but I remembered just before I left that my wife stole my Cardinals tee shirt. I thought I'd get back at her with this. She hates the Cowboys, but I went to high school with Danny White. Wearing this will really piss her off!" He laughed and shook his head. "Or at least she'll pretend to be mad. She went to school with him, too. We don't really fight…"

The man looked at his imaginary watch again. "It's way past beer thirty now! I'm outta here!"

"Thanks again," Arlie said, more grateful to the old guy than the man would ever know.

"So, someone really did give you the tokens to share?" Charlene asked, leaning close to Arlie so she didn't have to shout.

"I wouldn't lie to you," Arlie said, then took another sip of the coffee. "Ew! Well, I might trick you, but I never told you this coffee was good. I'd better throw it away before I take another drink without thinking."

Arlie stood up to throw away his drink, then realized that without his coffee, he had no reason to hang around. He reached into his pants pocket to get his keys, his gut aching at the thought of separation, when he felt it: one more token.

"Mommy, Mommy. Do you have any more coins for the carousel?" Chip asked, Carlos hanging onto his elbow, both boys' eyes wide with anticipation.

"Let me see... I have three left..."

"And I have one that I just found in my pocket," Arlie said. "Care to go on a trip around the world with me and the boys?"

"Come on, Mommy."

"Yeah, come on Chip's Mommy. We want you and Arlie to come, too. We're knights in shining armor and we're riding the horses, trying to catch up to the dragon this time. Last time we rode the dragon, but he's a bad dragon. You guys can be the king and queen and give us treasure when we cut off its head."

"Eww," Charlene said. "Can't you think of a better ending than that?"

"How about if you two herd the dragon with your lances so it finds its way back to dragon land," Arlie suggested. "Then he can be with his family again, too."

He held up his token, "Are you ready, Queen Arlene with a chuh?"

"I know the boys are, so why not, King Charlie without the chuh."

Chapter 8
Alice Cooper Therapy

Trivia: Although born in Michigan, the recording artist born Vincent Damon Furnier and now known as Alice Cooper, has adopted Arizona as his home. The music pioneer is credited with helping shape the shock rock music industry by both creating a new music style and incorporating fantastic visual presentations for his live performances.

***

Why didn't you ask her for her phone number, idiot? Not that you don't already have it, but she doesn't know that! That's what guys do when they're interested. Shit! You probably insulted her by not asking!

"Quit beating yourself up, Arlie," he said aloud. "Damned silence, anyhow." He reached over and turned on the radio, scanning stations until he found a heavy metal one. "Cool! An Alice Cooper marathon. There, that ought to drown out your frustrations and feelings of inadequacy." He turned up the volume until the Bug shuddered. "School's out!" he shouted, then reached over and rolled up the window to keep his solo rock concert private, "for summer!"

By the time he'd sung along to three of his favorite Alice

Cooper songs, Arlie had calmed down. He realized that time had flown and he was already at the stoplight just before his trailer park. He looked at the dashboard clock. "Crap. The samples haven't even hit Anchorage yet. I can't even call and bug her for two more hours, at least." His stomach churned, reminding him that he had skipped breakfast, and the small taste of spun fat and sugar that the barista passed off as a macchiato had left a foul taste in his mouth. Pizza was in the fridge, but a big bowl of cereal with a banana sliced on top sounded ideal. "Off to Sprawl-Mart, little Bug!"

Arlie added a bagged chopped cabbage salad kit to his hand basket of cereal, milk, and bananas, then decided to check out the bike section. Now that he'd been enlightened by the salesman at Pat's Bike Shop, he knew what to look for in a quality bicycle. It was time to see if his potential new employer had quality goods in stock.

"Arlie, right?"

"Oh, hi, Seth," Arlie said. "I guess you work weekends, then."

"Sometimes. Hey, did you get that email? I asked them to let you know as soon as possible. School's out now and parents are ordering bikes for Christmas like crazy. We're backed up with orders. You'll still have to go to the orientation, but that's on Monday and only for half a day. I was hoping you could start right after you were done with it. Well, after lunch, of course."

Arlie checked his email on his phone. "Where would it be coming from? No, wait, I found it. It wound up in the junk mail." He scanned the email. 'Welcome to the Sprawl-Mart family.' "Yes! I'm in. Thanks, Seth, for putting in a good word for me. I'm new in town and not having a job—or at least somewhere to go everyday where I'm needed—was getting on both the nerves I have left."

"Well, I'm glad we got it pushed through. Just make sure you show up on time Monday at 8:00 a.m. sharp. They'll set you up with all their legal forms, a name tag, and a vest. I have you penciled into the schedule for one o'clock. You'll have time to grab a bite, then I'll take you in the back where we put the bikes together. The first one will probably take a few hours, but after one or two more, you might be able to beat my record of forty-five minutes."

"Oh, Seth, you don't know what you're doing. I love a challenge. I'm not competitive with people, but I am with beating a record. Now, just so I'll know, do you ever sell these unassembled?"

Seth's shoulders worked back and forth, a sure sign to Arlie that he was leery about telling a secret, but if he did spill the beans, it would be the truth. "We try not to do that. If we do the assembly, we know it will be done right. There are so many complaints about missing parts or crappy instructions that corporate discovered it was cheaper in the long run to offer free assembly. That's why it's so important to have these bikes ready to roll out the door."

"So, if I bought one today, I could take it home and try my hand at figuring out the destructions?"

"Yeah, you got that right. The instructions for some of the models do seem more like destructions. Knock yourself out, but I'd wait until you're a full-blown employee so you can use your ten per-cent discount."

The phone at Seth's hip buzzed. "Hey, I gotta take this. See you Monday, Arlie."

Arlie waved good-bye to his young and affable new boss, then took a tour of the bicycles available. Cool! Stingrays, just what Chip wanted.

"Are you stalking me again," Charlene asked, then started laughing.

"What? Oh, hi, Charlene. Hi, Chip and Carlos." He sighed, then shook his head and smiled. "If I had seen you first, I would have asked the same question. No, I needed a few groceries," Arlie held up his basket of quick meals, "and decided to come back here and see what I was getting myself into."

"Getting yourself into? Explain…"

"I just got hired. I start working here on Monday afternoon. I'm the new bicycle assembly technician or whatever they call it. Anyhow, I'll take boxes of parts and tires and turn them into bikes and trikes for kids."

"And old folks," Charlene amended. "Haven't you seen all the seniors riding those big adult trikes?"

Arlie shook his head.

"Then you need to get out more. How long have you lived here?"

"Almost a week. Not having a job was driving me nuts. I can't stand to sit still."

"Mommy, Mommy," Chip said, pulling on her arm as soon as her conversation with Arlie had paused, "We forgot to get bananas and cereal" and pointed to Arlie's basket. "And do you think Carlos can spend the night again? And since school's out, he can come over to Angela's with me while you're at work!"

"Excuse me a minute," she said to Arlie. "Minor crisis," then turned to the two boys. "I'll check in with Rosa, but I'm sure she wants to see him, too. Maybe we can all get together for a picnic tomorrow? How does that sound?"

"Can Arlie come with us?" Chip asked.

"Yeah, can Arlie come with us?" Carlos echoed.

"Yeah, that'd be fun," Chip added. "If we go to the Lost Dutchman Park, I'll bet he can start a fire. We can roast weiners and marshmallows..."

Carlos giggled at the word weiners, then covered his mouth in a futile attempt to stifle it.

Chip turned to him. "Weiners and hot dogs are the same thing, sorta," and giggled, too. "At least, when you're having a picnic they are!"

"Let's see what Rosa's up to before we invite people, just in case we don't go."

"Make sure you get Arlie's phone number so you can call him and let him know. Please, please, even if Rosa doesn't want to go, you've been saying we'll go to Lost Dutchman for *ages*..." Chip said, drawing out the last word in an emotional plea for an extended play date.

"Okay. Arlie, can I get your number? I'll get with Rosa later. She's…um…occupied until this evening."

"All right. Here, I'll call my phone from yours." *If you call her from your phone, she might see that she's already in your contacts!*

Charlene handed him her wallet-cased phone and waiting while he called his own number, then hung up as soon as the number showed. "It says unknown, but that'll change as soon as you add me to your contacts."

Charlene took the phone from him, looked at his number, then stared at him. "You're from Alaska?"

"Yup, I'm a snowbird. I may or may not go back, but I'm definitely here until the sidewalks are ice-free," he said, then grimaced. *Why would you say that, idiot? Now she might figure out you're physically limited, that you can't walk on slippery surfaces or have some other major defect.*

Chip took advantage of the break in the adults' conversation. "That's the bike I want, Mommy," pointing to the one Arlie had been looking at. "Just like that one, but with that seat," and indicated the gold-flecked banana seat with the exaggerated sissy bar in back.

"We'll see, honey. I think the economy's been rough on Santa this year."

"Huh?" Chip asked, mouth opened in confusion.

"I think Santa's broke, too. Come on, let's go get more cereal and bananas. With two of you around, food disappears twice as fast."

Charlene looked over at Arlie, her eyes squinted in uncertainty. "I'll call you later when I find out about tomorrow," she said.

"Even if Carlos can't come," Arlie replied, trying to bring the conversation back up its former brightness, "I'd like to go. I've heard about the Lost Dutchman, but didn't know there was a park for him. Oh, and I'm a dandy fire-starter, an Eagle Scout and all that good stuff."

"Eagle Scout," she said and nodded her head, his thin personal resume suddenly taking on a healthy weight. "All right. I'll let you know this evening."

Chapter 9
The Lost Dutchman

Travel brochure item: Lost Dutchman State Park is a 320-acre state park located near the Superstition Mountains, a short drive east from Mesa, Arizona. It was named after Jacob Waltz, a 19th-century German gold miner whose legendary treasure has never been found.

***

"Yes, ma'am, go ahead and give me the extended warranty on the bike. Just in case."

Arlie paid for his basic food supplies and the project that he hoped would keep his brain occupied until Abby received and tested the DNA samples he had sent her the night before.

Put the bags and boxes in the back of the Beetle, then head on home to Santa's Southern Workshop. Looks like jolly St. Nick got a Christmas bonus and will be able to deliver that bike to Chip after all. With matching banana seats for both boys, too!

Okay. Check your watch. How long will it take you to get home? Might as well figure travel time now. You don't want to be late for work the first day!

It wasn't until Arlie was in his combo living room-dining room and had pulled all the bike parts out of the box that he realized he still hadn't eaten. "Crap! I forgot to buy bowls! All right, what do you have…"

Arlie looked in all the cupboards, then spied the saucepan he had bought to heat up canned soup. "That'll do."

He was in the middle of eating his mega-serving of frosted cornflakes and sliced bananas when his phone rang.

Charlene. Sweet!

"Good afternoon, Charlene."

"How… Oh, yeah. You put me in your contacts. Hey, I just called Rosa. She texted me that she couldn't talk right now, but to go ahead and keep Carlos another night; she'd pick him up Sunday evening sometime."

"All right. Does that mean it's just you and me and the boys for a picnic tomorrow?" *Hope, hope!*

"Yeah, I guess so…"

"Hey, I got an idea," Arlie said, trying to change her dour tone to one of anticipation at a day off in the mountains. "How about if you meet me in the Sprawl-Mart parking lot, on the side where the water bottle fill station is? There's no reason to take two vehicles, so if you don't mind driving…"

"I don't mind at all. Plus, I know where I'm going and you don't. I'll be in a white Subaru Outback."

"You should be easy to find."

"You can tell you haven't been here long. Or maybe you just didn't notice that about 80% of the vehicles here are white."

"Yes, I did notice it, but not many white station wagons are carrying two red-headed boys. Oh, and by the way, I have an ice chest. I can fill it with soda and hot dogs…or *weiners*…"

Charlene laughed as he repeated the boys' giggle-producing word and waited for her response.

"Anyhow, what kind should I buy? Do you have condoms… I mean, condiments?"

"Arlie! Where'd you get that sense of humor? Yes, I'll bring the condom…ments and a can of baked beans. Oh, and a small pan to heat them in. Any kind of, eh hem, hot dogs will do. Anything else?"

"Yeah, I'll bring paper plates and plastic utensils. I have plenty here. What I don't have are real dishes. I'm eating my cereal out of a saucepan!"

Charlene laughed at the visual of him holding a pan with

one hand, a plastic spoonful of cereal and sliced bananas with the other. "You're too funny. How about 11:00? No, wait, we should go sooner. How early are you willing to go?"

Arlie paused, thinking about how much time he should give Abby to finish her diagnostics. He realized that Alaska was two hours earlier than Arizona in the winter. "It doesn't make a difference to me. I don't have much of anything to do here. I already finished my fleecy pillow cover." He looked at the parts and wheels sprawled all over the floor and into the kitchen. "I just have one small do-it-yourself kit to put together, but I should be done with that in an hour or two."

"Well, after the boys eat their cereal and bananas for breakfast, brush their teeth... Let's say meet at the water bottle filler-upper machine at 8:30."

"Sounds great to me."

"Okay, 8:30. I'll bring some sunscreen, too. You're pretty fair-skinned, so you might want to wear a hat, too."

"Got it. Red hair and sunshine, a sure combination for sunburn."

"Yeah, well, as Chip's mother, I found that out a long time ago. He's not as bad as some redheads, though. Probably the brown eyes. Bye."

And there you have it, Slick. You have a date with the mother of one of your children and with both of your boys. A week ago, you didn't even know Carlos existed. Does it get any finer than this?

Arlie readjusted his jeans and realized that a part of him had become excited. "Quit that," he said, then tried to squelch its physical manifestation by pushing it down. It popped up, even firmer and more insistent. "Okay, you win. Sort of. No cold shower this time, but I'm changing into basketball shorts so I can get this bike built in under 45 minutes."

***

"What's wrong, Mommy. You look sad," Chip said. "I thought you'd be happy to go on a picnic."

"I am, dear. I'm sorry, it's just that I have a lot on my mind." Charlene looked over at Carlos and saw he looked bummed, too. "Are you okay, honey?"

"Yeah, I just miss my mom. Before we moved here, she used to have to go away for long times and leave me with my nanny, but she always came back. I hope she's okay. Can I talk to her?"

"I'll call her again. Just a minute."

Charlene put her reusable grocery bag away, then sat on the couch, patting the seat beside her for Carlos to join her. She let the phone ring until it went to the generic voice mail that came with Rosa's phone. "Hmm. Let's try again in a couple minutes. Maybe she stepped away or something."

"Yeah, like went potty or something," Chip said. He came over and sat close to Carlos, then put his arm around his almost twin's shoulder. "It's going to be okay. My mom's better than any nanny. You can stay with us as long as you want, huh, Mommy?"

Charlene knelt down beside the boys and hugged both of them at the same time. "Yes, you can stay with us as long as your mother needs us to watch you. Even if she isn't busy, you're welcome here."

"Good," Carlos said. "Because I like it here a lot. My house is too big, even if it is smaller than my old house. Besides, no one yells here. I think I like that the best!"

***

"Crap! Three hours and forty-five minutes! Damned instructions anyhow. I'll bet they were written in Chinese, translated into Japanese, then translated into English. No wonder Sprawl-Mart has them assembled *professionally*! I sure hope Seth has a few pointers…or better instructions."

Arlie got up off the floor and saw that he had one three-inch screw left over. "That's not good." He set it on the counter, then groaned and stretched his back, "I'll deal with spare parts later. I'm putting that brace back on, then going for a walk. By the time I return, it'll be time to call Abby."

Zippidee doo dah! Zippidee…."

Arlie snatched the phone out of his shirt pocket. "Hello, Abby! I was going to call you later. What's my girl got for me today?"

"Do you still have that stupid ring tone set for me?" Abby asked.

"You know I do, darlin'. So, what did you find out?"

"I just wanted to call you before you got too wound up. Yes, I got the package and yes, the samples were good. I'm running the DNA quantitation now. I should know how much DNA is in the samples you sent in an hour or so. But, you do remember that I still need about six hours to add juice to it and run it through the PCR. And then," she said and took a deep breath, "I have to run it through the 310 to see if whomever is in the database."

"Abby, I love you and I know you know what you're doing,

but genetic profiling was an eight-hour class I took years ago. You're speaking Martian. Bottom line is you should have results for me when?"

"About midnight my time which means about two in the morning for you. Are you sure you want me to call you then?"

"Absolutely! You know you can call me any day or time…"

"Cut the crap, Arlie. I know this is important to you because you've never asked me to do anything like this before. I just want to know: when this is all done, are you going to tell me what this is all about or will I know when I see the results?"

"I will let you know. It might be a couple days before I can get my research done after you verify the women's names, but I promise I'll let you know."

"All right. Now, I have things to do. I'd say what a crappy way to spend a Saturday night, but I don't have a girlfriend and it's snowing again. I'm glad you're there. The sidewalks are horrid! Even ice cleats and two canes wouldn't work in these conditions!"

"I'm glad I'm here, too. Talk to you in the morning."

"Yeah, the very early morning."

***

"Hullo? Oh, yeah, I'm awake. Sorta. What did you find?"

"Didn't you tell me that these were from women?"

"Yeah. I had one marked 'C' and one 'R'. Why? Is there a problem?"

"Well, other than the fact that both of these are from males, yeah, and double yeah."

"Hold on a sec." Arlie sat up straight, took a swig from his bedside water bottle to clear his head, and asked, "Would you say that again, but in a different way? I heard the words but they didn't make sense."

"All right. First off, the samples are from males, not females. No doubt about that. However, since this was so important to you, I broke it down even further. I guess I let my mind run wild, trying to figure out what you were…"

"Abby, pardon my French, but cut the crap."

"Congratulations, Arlie, you have two sons!" Abby said, then giggled. "I'm sorry. There wasn't a gentle way to tell you. These are two different males, to be sure, but even if they were your brother's children, they wouldn't be so full of your DNA. Why didn't you just ask for a paternity test? That would have been a lot easier."

"Shit…"

"Arlie… Did you know you had two sons?"

"I kinda sorta knew about one of them. I didn't know about the other one until Friday night. So, can you tell anything on the maternal side of them?"

"Well, since I had my suspicions early on with you wanting to get a paternity test on the down low, I ran you first. Sorry. Or not. It made everything else a lot easier. I knew you were from around here, so I started with the Alaska database. Zing! You got one sweetheart of a mommy and another, as you call her, a bad pajama mama."

"Names, please?"

"First, Arlie, were you really that promiscuous that you have sons from two different women and you don't even know their names?"

"Abby, in order to keep you from fantasizing about my sex life any more than you already have, I'll tell you what happened. But do not tell anyone on pain of severe and horrific payback, all right?"

"Cross my heart and hope to be the butt of your insane paybacks for two years."

"I was a sperm donor seven years ago. It was actually a

bit of a college prank. I didn't use my own name but did get curious soon afterwards. Now some 'stuff' has happened and I want to make sure the boy—or boys, as I found out two days ago—aren't hurt."

"Okay. Mom number one is Charlene Barbour. As a first lieutenant, she was attached to Fort Richardson JAG. She left after her tour of duty to start a family and relocated to Phoenix, Arizona. She now resides in Mesa, Arizona and is involved in a rather nasty discrimination suit against her former employers."

"I got that one, Abby. Now, how about the other one? You said you started with Alaska. Is it someone I might know?"

"I'll refrain from jokes about you not knowing the mother of your children," Abby said, then giggled. "Sorry, I'm punch drunk from being up so late, but you said you wanted the results ASAP."

"The other one…"

"Well, you may not know the mother, but you're pretty close to her husband. Or were. Her name is Carla Rosa Romano De Luca. Her husband is Alonzo De Luca, the guy who shot you."

"Yeah, I seem to remember his name," Arlie said dryly.

"Crap. Any more on Carla?"

"Back in the day, she'd give you a run for your skills in cyber sleuthing. She fell off the radar six years ago. Rumor is she moved to Costa Rica, but that bit of intel was based on one of our operatives actually seeing her. She's still off the radar."

"She's in Mesa, Arizona right now. Or she was Friday night when she got drunk and was hanging all over me at a pizza parlor. Does she have any warrants out?"

"Nope, she's sparkling from what I could see. I wouldn't doubt that she cleaned up her own record, though. She started early, logging into school servers and changing her grades. She seems to like to make herself look good. She's never been malicious that I can find."

"But if there was something out there, she probably cleaned it up, right?"

"Right. Arlie, I'd love to stay and talk to you, but usually if I'm on the phone this late at night, it's for phone sex. And quite frankly, your voice is too low to turn me on."

"I could talk like this," Arlie said in a falsetto voice, then dropped down to his normal tone. "You really are the best, Abby. Take care. If I need anything else, I'll go through channels."

"Arlie, there's only one thing I want from you, maybe two. Would you send me pictures of your sons, and maybe their mothers?"

"I'll see what I can do. I have a date with Charlene and the boys tomorrow." Arlie paused. "No, wait, I have a date with them in a few hours. I need to get some rest. Love ya, lady!"

"Love you, too, Arlie. G'night."

Arlie set his phone back on the charger. One o'clock in the morning. It didn't take her as long as she thought. Or her little sniggling suspicions cut down the research time…

Charlene and Rosa must have been holding the cups for their sons. Oh, well. Same questions answered; it was just more work for Abby. The alarm is set on the phone, so get some sleep. Dad.

***

"Crap!"

Arlie rolled out of bed, his back twinging at the irritation of waking up late. It was 7:30. He had to shower, hide the bike—just in the off chance he had visitors—and then rush to Sprawl-Mart to get an ice chest, sodas, buns and hot dogs.

"Weiners," he said, then chuckled at his own sausage that

was begging for attention. "One of these days, dude. Even self-gratification could move that bullet around. Damned Alonzo!"

A quick washing of the important parts of his body with tepid water calmed down the bit that needed relaxing the most and energized the rest of him. "Let's see... Bike and extra seats stashed in the bedroom, no dirty dishes in the sink... All righty then. Nothing to take but me and my phone." He saw the tell-tale spare bolt from the bicycle and shoved it in his pocket. "Not that anyone would know what it is, even if they did show up."

***

"Mommy, Mommy, there's Arlie," the boys said when they saw him coming out of the store.

Charlene gave Carlos a quizzical look for calling her Mommy.

"Hey, he calls you Mommy—why can't I? He can call my mama 'Mama' like I do. She won't mind."

A feigned smile crossed Charlene's chin, her eyes still worried that something had happened to her new friend.

"Boys, would you put the cans of soda in the ice chest for me?" Arlie asked. "Gently, though, or they'll spray all over the place when we open them."

The boys looked at each other, the mischievous twinkles in their eyes impossible to miss. "And if it makes a mess and sprays all over the place, there won't be any left to drink," he added.

Frowns took over their impish grins, then they set to work, one taking the cans out of the box, the other setting them gently into the ice chest.

"What's wrong?" Arlie asked Charlene softly, keeping an eye on his helpers.

"It's Rosa. I only talked to her on Friday night, and for half of that she was snockered." She looked at Arlie who shrugged his shoulder. "Yeah, that's right. You were there. She was stressed, though, big time. She drives a fancy Maserati. We left it at her place after the school carnival and before the pizza parlor so she could have a drink. When we came back, it had been moved. She said her soon-to-be ex-husband is the only one who had another key. She was sooo careful going into that house. She even held her shirt over the handle like she was afraid it was poisoned or something. I came in to check on her when she didn't come back out right away. She said everything was okay, that she was probably just being paranoid. She let me take Carlos to spend the night—said she had a good book to read—and we swapped phone numbers.

"I called her the next morning. She didn't answer, but right afterwards, I got a text from her saying she had an appointment and that she'd pick him up later."

Arlie nodded, waiting for her to add more. He didn't want to seem to eager, then realized that being a detective had nothing to do with concern about a missing mother. "I think…

"Arlie, can we help you put the ice in?" Chip asked.

"Sure. Just a minute." He turned to Charlene. "Let me think about what you said for a minute. This is just too crazy for real life." He pulled his knife out of his pocket and sliced the top off the bag of ice.

"Ready boys? I'll pour and you spread it around."

"Did you get marshmallows, Arlie?" Charlene asked and gave him a subtle wink, eager to break away and make another phone call.

"Yeah, I did, but I think we'll need two. Boys, do you think we can eat two bags of marshmallows today?"

The two jumped up and down with excitement, screaming, 'Yeah! Yeah!"

"Go ahead, Charlene. I got this," and waved her away.

"Okay, boys, let's set the *wieners* on top of everything else, then we can play a game."

The boys giggled on cue, then helped him organize the cold food on top of the ice. The three of them repacked Charlene's reusable grocery bag with some of the goodies Arlie had bought, both boys eager to have time with the first man who had shown attention to them in their lives.

"So, do you guys know when your birthdays are? Mine's October 24. Chip, when's yours?"

"Mine's June 21st. When's yours Carlos?"

"Mine's June 22nd, so I'm a day older."

"No," Arlie said. "The date is higher, but that means you were born the day after he was. He was a day old when you were born. Now, do you boys know your mothers' names? It's very important to know your mother and father's name in case you get lost."

"My mother's name is Charlene Barbour and I was named after her. I don't know about my father. She said that's not important. One day I might have a daddy, and that's lots more important than having a father."

"Me, me, me, too! I was named after my mother, too! Her

name is Carla Rosa Romano De Luca, but right now, she said that her name in Arizona is Rosa Smith." Carlos let out an exaggerated sigh. "That's sure a lot easier to say!"

"What about your father, Carlos?" Arlie asked, making mental notes of his game-playing interrogation.

"He's Alonzo De Luca," he said, then spat on the ground.

"Whoa! Carlos, it's rude to spit," Arlie said.

"That's what my mama does when she says his name…"

"Well, I'm sure she has her reasons, but let's not spit, all right?" Arlie saw Carlos frown at being reprimanded. "Unless you got a bug in your mouth or something," he said, then added *pbbt, pbbt, pbbt!*

The boys giggled, then copied his less emphatic spitting technique.

"I'm back," Charlene said, another forced smile on her face. "Do you have everything ready?"

The boys bounced up and down and cheered, "Yeah, yeah! Let's go!"

"Okay, everyone. Seatbelts! Let's go see if we can find the Lost Dutchman's gold!" she said, then climbed in the driver's seat.

Chapter 10
Unidentified Female

Late breaking news. A 2010 Maserati Quattroporte was found burning in a dry wash east of Apache Junction by a jogger early this morning. The sole female occupant did not survive the apparent one-vehicle accident. Alcohol is believed to be a factor. The incident is under investigation. Identification pending notification of next of kin.

***

Arlie looked behind him, saw Carlos had plenty of leg room, then scooted his seat back. He felt for the lever on the side, then reclined back. "First class accommodations," he said. "Thanks," and shut his eyes, a smile of bliss on his face.

"Rough night last night?" Charlene asked, not even trying to hide the tease in her voice.

"Nope. Last night was great. It was an early morning phone call that sort of messed me up. I'll be fine. I wouldn't miss this for anything. This is *way* better than making up a couple hours of missed sleep in a tuna can-sized trailer in an old folks RV park."

"Yeah, I saw where you're staying. I watched you pull in there yesterday. It's clean and safe, though. What more could anyone ask?"

Arlie looked at her and winked, but didn't say a word, then returned to his kicked back demeanor.

Flirting with her now, are you? Not even trying to hide your desire? Be cool, dude. You don't want to scare her away! She's your only link to those boys. If you piss her off, you'll never see them anywhere except on surveillance video!

"I'm sorry. That came across as crude. What I meant was it would be nice if it my place was a lot bigger and didn't cost so much per square foot." He frowned and tried to make a joke. "Of course, if it *was* bigger, it would cost even more."

"The only way to get more for less in this part of the world is to move further out into the desert. If you're willing to live off the grid with solar power and tote in your own water, you can get a decent-sized piece of property. You might even be able to afford enough land to raise a few goats and chickens."

"Sounds to me, Charlene, like you've thought about that a lot. Is that what you'd do if you had the money from..." He quickly bit off the words 'your discrimination settlement.' *Shut up about winning a legal case you're not supposed to know about!*

Arlie feigned a cough. "Excuse me. If you had money from the death of some distant relative you didn't even know?"

"Yeah, probably. I'd rather work hard at making hens and kids thrive than scanning sheet sets and toothbrushes." She tipped her head back to indicate Chip. "I'd even be willing to home school *that* kid," and laughed. "It would nice to look forward to going to town once or twice a month. Right now, it's shuffle him off to school or to a sitter five days a week, playing beat the clock and rush hour traffic to make sure my life fits into someone else's agenda. When is it going to be our time?"

"Um, I don't know…"

"Sorry. I don't get the chance to rant very often. I guess that's the price you have to pay for first class accommodations." She took her eyes off the road and smiled at him. "You're a good listener. So, what would you do if you had all the time and money you could want?"

Find the best surgeon in the world and have him take that mother-f'ing bullet out of my back! Arlie cleared his throat as he thought about what would be second on his list. "Shoot!" He squirmed in his seat, then sat up. "I never thought much about it, but it sounds like you have Eden just about figured out. Except maybe find a piece of land where you could sink a well and wouldn't have to haul in water. Plus, I think I'd want to go to a higher altitude. I may not be too fond of snow anymore, but a change of seasons would be nice. Christmas is only a week away, and I really think snow should be part of the picture, at least at some point."

"Hey, Mommy are we going to the Stupidstitious Mountains?" Chip asked.

"Superstition Mountains, and yes, that's where Lost Dutchman Park is. We went there this summer, but we didn't stay long because it was too hot. It's cool enough now that we can take a hike before we eat. I have water bottles in my backpack and we're all wearing tennis shoes, so we're set. It's too early for lunch plus we need to work up an appetite."

Arlie's stomach growled at the mention of food. He hadn't had time for breakfast. Charlene leaned close to him and said, "Open the glovebox and grab a granola bar without them seeing. We all ate, but it sounds like you didn't."

"Boys, what's the name of that mountain again?" Arlie asked.

As soon as they chorused 'Stupidstitions,' he snagged the granola bar and shoved it in the leg pocket of his cargo pants.

"Superstious, I mean Superstition," Charlene said, then laughed. "Well, at least you got the last half right. We'll work on it together, boys."

***

"We're here!" Charlene said, and pulled up near the picnic tables. "Why don't you boys play catch or something for a few minutes while Arlie and I set up, okay?"

"Yes, Mommy," they said, then giggled.

"Go long, Chip," Charlene called and cocked her arm to throw the foam mini football.

Chip missed the easy throw and said, "You throw like a girl, Mommy!" then the two boys scrambled to retrieve it.

"I can't help it, but I'll work on it," she said brightly, then turned to Arlie.

"I need to talk to you and I didn't want the boys around." She set her backpack on the picnic table, then looked inside, moving aside the water bottles, looking for something. She brought out a Taurus PT1111 gun.

"Whoa! You're hiding a gun?"

"Don't worry, it's legal and so am I." She put it back in the inside side pocket, but left that part unzipped. "Don't let the boys get their own water."

"So, what's going on? Are you afraid of rattlesnakes or something?" Arlie asked, not sure whether he should make a joke out of his comment and laugh or not. He decided not to.

"Yes, I'm afraid of rattlesnakes, but it's the *or something* that has me glad I brought a gun. The last time I heard from Rosa was Friday night after I dropped her off and she asked me to take Carlos for the night. She called me after the boys went to sleep. She said she made an appointment with a friend who said he'd make sure she never had to worry about Alonzo again. She was meeting with the guy Saturday morning. I told her to be careful—it sounded fishy to me. I even told her that her judgment might be impaired by the wine she had, but she shrugged it off by saying, 'I want to be rid of him for good.'

"'But he's the boy's father,' I said, hoping to sway her so she wouldn't do something she could get the death penalty for. 'He's not his father,' she said, then I heard her spit. She apologized, then told me the story.

"She got into some legal trouble when she was younger and Alonzo pulled some strings or threw money around—she wasn't sure—and got her record cleaned. She was grateful, but not that grateful! He was big and ugly and had horrible body odor. Then he started lavishing gifts on her, including the Maserati she's still driving. Well, she said she developed gold blindness. She figured she'd marry him in a community property state and stay there for a while, then get a divorce.

"Of course, that's not what he wanted. He was Italian and wanted a big family right away. She said she stayed drunk for almost a year to be able to tolerate his sexual appetite. He'd jump on her at least twice, sometimes three times a day, trying to get her pregnant. She even went to the doctor to make sure she wasn't the problem. She knew better than to suggest he was sterile or had a low wiggler count. Her plan was to go somewhere Alonzo wouldn't want to go and get artificially inseminated there. She told him, 'The doctor said I wasn't getting pregnant because I was stressed and needed a vacation. Plus, if I abstain from sex for a week or two, I'll be super fertile when I get back from holiday.'

"He knew she had already been on fertility drugs for three months, so he let her go, hoping the doctor's latest suggestion would work. He sent a bodyguard with her, but he was no problem. Rosa said she just paid him to sit at the titty bar all day and get lap dances. She had already contacted the *spunk bank*, as she called it, and got the donor picked out. She said she'd pay cash when she got there. Well, it turns out the clinic had a power failure and all the records were lost. 'Just give me the juice from someone with an Italian name.'

I guess the new receptionist was both young and naïve. 'I don't know what an Italian name sounds like and I'm not supposed to tell you the donor, anyway.' Rosa gave her a couple hundred-dollar bills and said, 'Start reading, honey.' She stopped her when she got to the name Jake Spinelli. That's why she just about fainted when you said that name at the winter carnival."

Arlie shifted in his seat and his stomach roared. "I guess I should eat something," he said.

"No, you should tell me what's going on. Your body language is confirming what my suspicions are. Why did you ask her about Jake Spinelli?"

"He was my college roommate," Arlie said, then reached into his leg pocket for the granola bar. *Yeah, tell her the truth. If she was with JAG then worked as a legal secretary, she's got experience with watching for tells from liars.*

The oat and candy bar tasted like busted up plywood in

his mouth, but he chewed and swallowed, aware that she was waiting for him to say more.

"Did you ever wonder why Carlos and Chip looked so much alike?" Charlene asked, goading him into revealing how much he knew and she suspected.

Her blunt question took him totally by surprise and he started to cough. "What?" he managed to ask, his face crimson from both the question and from nearly choking on the nutty bits that went down the wrong way.

"I've never been married," Charlene said. "I was engaged, though. I was stationed at Fort Richardson, Alaska. My fiancé, Otto Russo, was stationed there, too. Even though he was twelve years older than me, I thought we had a great relationship. I found out too late that he was both a liar and the scum on the bottom of pond scum. But I digress.

"Because he was older, Otto wanted a big family right away. There was a problem, though. He said he'd had mumps when he was younger and was therefore sterile. We made the decision together for insemination. 'Just get someone with Italian heritage. No one will be the wiser,' he said. I was willing to go through all the hormone shots to make me super fertile. I'd be pregnant when we got married—just after I got out of the service—but I didn't care.

"Two days after I became intimately acquainted with a medical-grade turkey baster, he got shipped to Afghanistan. A week later, he was dead."

"Oh, I'm so sorry…" Arlie said, genuinely sad for her loss.

She shrugged one shoulder. "I was upset, to be sure. I didn't know what to do, but I was carrying his baby, at least in name. He was going to be Otto Russo, Junior. My dad lived in Anchorage and was very supportive. 'I'll help you with whatever you need. You'll be out of the army when the baby's born and we can raise him together."

"That's so sweet. Having a great father is such a treasure."

Charlene eyes narrowed in a threatening scowl, so he scooted back on the bench and let her finish without any more interruptions.

"A month later, I found out that Otto wasn't killed in action. He had deserted his post and was killed while trying to make a drug deal with the Taliban. The next day, his wife showed up on post with their five kids, looking for survivor benefits. He wasn't sterile, that's for sure! He had it all figured out. If I had a surrogate's baby that he never legally adopted, then he would never have to pay child support, plus we wouldn't actually be married because he already had a wife. The wannabe bigamist had a plan, all right.

"I was beyond upset and half-crazed from the hormones. Shoot! I was all set to get an abortion so I wouldn't have a reminder of him or what I thought we had. But then I realized that this was my baby, too. I went to the first doctor's appointment to confirm I was pregnant. I knew I was, but still, I went. They did an ultrasound. There were two fetuses! I was so excited! Any thoughts of abortion went out with the trash.

Arlie bit his bottom lip, glowing at the thought of how happy she must have been at that time, then frowned. He had missed it.

Charlene saw Arlie's mixed emotions and realized she was conflicted, too. There was a very good chance that he was the father of her son, and of Rosa's son, too. He had missed out and was feeling remorse. Mark that down as a bonus point in the character evaluation.

"The next visit, there was only one fetus. The technician told me that happens occasionally. In the first trimester, one of the multiples dies and the mother's body absorbs it."

Arlie shuddered, but didn't speak.

"So, that's why when I see Chip and Carlos together, it's so special for me. He's the twin I never got."

Charlene's face softened as she saw Arlie in a different light. How many men donated sperm anonymously and never gave it a second thought. He had shuddered and blushed and sighed at all the right spots. He may not have been there when Chip was born, but she'd give him a shot at being there for the rest of his life.

"Mommy, Mommy. Can you get the ball for us? It went all the way over there..." Chip said and pointed across the access road.

"I'll get it," Arlie said, and stood up and stretched. "My back...I mean, I need a moment. You need to hear something, and I want to make sure I say this right."

"Here's your sons' ball," the blond young man on the mountain bike said and tossed the ball to Arlie. "Geez, they look just like you. I'm a twin, too. My brother and I looked like Dad. Folks used to say we were triplets, but that he was born twenty-five years earlier."

"Thanks for the ball," Arlie said, and waved to the cyclist.

Yup, it's that obvious. You'd better make it right with Charlene. And the sooner the better!

"Here you go, boys," Arlie said and tossed it six feet straight up in the air. "Let your mom and me talk for a few more minutes, then we can climb all the way up to the top of that!" and pointed to the peak.

"Goodie, goodie!" Carlos said.

"And when we come back, you can make a fire and we can cook marshmallows!" Chip added.

"After we cook the other food…" Arlie said with laugh.

"Wieners, wieners," the boys said, then ran toward the playground area where retrieving stray throws would be easier.

"So," Arlie said, then sat down across from Charlene.

She finished cleaning under her fingernail and looked up. "So…" she prompted.

"I guess the easiest way is to just blurt it out. Yes, I highly suspect that I'm the father of both Chip and Carlos." Arlie took a deep breath as he sat up straight. "That's the easy part, I suppose. I can apologize, but then I see those boys and I'm so happy you and Rosa got to be mothers… I just feel rotten that we couldn't do it the old-fashioned way."

"Excuse me?" Charlene asked coldly, her tone indignant, her rage barely contained. Maybe she had been too quick to give him bonus points for empathy.

Arlie looked at her, wondering why she was so upset, then it dawned on him. "No! No, no, no! I didn't mean the sex part! I meant the traditional family part. You know, get introduced by a mutual friend, go on a hundred dates or twelve, get married, have a child together, I'd go to all the doctor's appointments with you, hold your hand while you pushed him out… That's what I was talking about."

"All right. I can see that's what you really meant. So, why did you do it? Did they pay you?"

"I only did it once, and yes, I got paid. My roommate was a pain in the ass sometimes. I had borrowed a few hundred bucks when funds were tight. He kept bugging me about it, wanting it before I got my PFD. You know, the Permanent Fund Dividend—the reverse income tax? Oh, that's right, you lived in Alaska and know all about it. Anyhow, I went to the sperm bank, gave them his name," Arlie blushed crimson, a sharp contrast to his auburn red hair, "made my deposit, then left. They mailed the check to the address and name I had given them. He got paid back and never bothered me again. Except he stole my girlfriend. I never did thank him for that…"

"So, how come you're here now?" Charlene asked, then

stood up to make sure the boys were still occupied.

"The real Jake Spinelli called and said someone robbed the sperm bank and evidently was looking for the donor by that name. A man called him, said he had found a wallet with that name inside and wanted to get it back to the owner. Jake admitted that was his name. He didn't trust the guy, so set up the meeting at the mall. He never got close, just hid and watched as two men scared the piss out of the wrong guy. He overheard them say they were going to kill that red-headed bastard father, then off the mother and child, too. When he told me about it, I figured I'd better step in and make sure you were safe."

"Me? Why me?"

"You were the only mother I knew of. Carla Romano had disappeared. I thought she was dead or never had the child, although I knew she had been impregnated."

"How and why did you know that?"

"I'm a cop. An Anchorage undercover detective. And now, after a bit more research, I know for sure that both Carlos and Chip are my sons. And that Rosa is really Carla De Luca, the wife of Alonzo De Luca, the man who tried to kill me six months ago."

"Mommy! Mommy! I wanna go up there, please! You said we were going to go on a hike and all you're doing is talking to Arlie…"

"Yeah, just talking to Arlie," Carlos added, trying to out-pout Chip.

"All right, all right," Charlene said, then zipped up the backpack. "To the bathroom, boys, then we'll go." She turned to Arlie. "To be continued."

"Absolutely, to be continued," Arlie replied. "Come on, boys, over here. This side is for girls."

***

After twenty minutes of steep climbing, Charlene slowed down to be at Arlie's side. "There's something else I just remembered. I got so wound up with the paternity talk, I forgot to tell you. I made a real dumb mistake just before we left Sprawl-Mart. I called Rosa's phone. Again. I left another message, telling her that I was taking the boys to Lost Dutchman Park. As soon as the words left my lips, I realized that if someone—like her soon-to-be ex-husband—had her phone or was monitoring it, I had just informed him where to find Carlos. I quickly added, 'Unless we decide to go to the movies.'"

"As soon as we get in cell range," Arlie said, "file a missing persons report. She's been gone twenty-four hours, or close enough, right?"

"Yeah, and Carlos told Chip that his father wanted to kill him and his mother. I guess his father's hatred is no big secret."

"Thanks for letting me know."

Arlie turned to the boys. "There's the top. We're almost there. Come on! Let's go get a picture, shall we?" He turned to Charlene and said, "There's nothing we can do about it now but be careful."

All four of them scrambled to the top. "Here, Arlie. Take a picture of me and the boys with my phone," Charlene said, and handed him her phone.

"Do you want me to take a picture of the whole family?" asked the athletic young woman, already done with her climb.

"Yes, would you? And get one with both phones, if you don't mind," Arlie added, then handed her his phone.

Snap! Snap! The lady put Charlene's phone in her pocket and took out Arlie's. *Snap-snap-snap-snap-snap-snap-snap!*

"What the heck?" she asked, looking at it to make sure

she hadn't broken it.

"Burst shot," he said, "Just in case one of us had eyes closed. Thanks! Do you want a picture of you with this background?"

"No, thanks, I come up here almost every day."

Zippidee Doo Dah, Zippidee Day!

"Here, I think your phone is calling you," she said and handed it back to him.

Arlie quickly pushed the answer button, said, "Thanks," to the athlete in training, then moved further up the rise.

"Hey, Abby. What's going on?"

"Where in the hell have you been? I've been calling you for over half an hour. I just about wore out the redial button."

"I just got in cell phone range. We're climbing Superstition Mountain, or part of it."

"Who's we?"

"Charlene, the boys, and me. And again, what's going on?"

"Oh!" she said, excited that he was with his sons, then added a somber, "oh," when she realized she had to be the one to break the bad news. "Arlie, the De Lucas are on the loose."

"Yeah, well tell me something I didn't know."

"All right. They killed Carla or Rosa or whatever you call her. Or probably did. The local cops found her burned-out car and said alcohol was involved. I had flagged her name as a person of interest in the database, so when they matched her DNA, I was notified. Sorry, but she's dead."

Arlie slumped against the boulder behind him. "Crap. Carlos needs a parent."

"Well, you're one. It's easy enough to prove with a paternity test, but it's going to be hard to explain why and how."

Arlie swiped and tapped on his phone. "You can see my location now, Abby. Do you have a fix on where they found Rosa's car? How close am I to it?"

"Hmm. Let's see… As the crow flies, you're about fifteen miles away. Arlie, it's a good possibility that those crazy brothers are close by…"

"Yeah, well, it gets even worse. Charlene accidentally spilled the beans on a voice mail to Rosa about where we were going to be this morning. Rosa probably didn't get the word, but the De Lucas probably did. If you don't hear from me in an hour, call the Pinal County Sheriff's office and tell them there's been a murder."

"Arlie! No!"

"Don't worry, Abby. I'm not saying they're going to kill me, but do you think they'd come investigate if you said there were bad guys on the loose? Right now, I don't even know if they have any evidence on who set her car on fire. Letting them know the whole backstory would take too long and would be time wasted when they could be on their way."

"Okay, I set my timer. Would you do me a favor, though?"

"Anything for you, darlin'."

"Send me a picture of the boys…"

"I'll do even better. Watch your email for a family picture. Love, ya, Lady A."

Arlie hit end, then scrolled through the images shot moments ago. "Here you go, sweetie…" he said under his breath.

"So, was that your girlfriend?" Charlene asked, suddenly at his elbow.

"What? No, no way." He realized his last few words on the phone probably sounded a little friendly. "You just caught the tail end of a conversation. That was Abby, the lady who runs the crime lab in downtown Anchorage." He shrugged his shoulder and smiled. "She'd be a great candidate for a girlfriend or even a wife, but…"

Arlie waited for a scowl of jealousy before telling her more. And then it appeared—starting out as confusion, but definitely ending up as the green-eyed monster. "She said my voice was too low for her and I had too much plumbing. Or maybe it was because it was on the outside."

"Wait. What? Too much… Oh, she likes other girls… So, if you don't mind me asking, what was that all about. By the frown on your face when you started talking to her, I thought someone had died. Then you wound up being all sassy and happy."

"Here, sit down." Arlie stood away from her and watched to make sure the boys were still safe. "Don't throw rocks! There are people down there." He turned back to her. "Rosa's dead. The cops found her car, burnt to a crisp. Word is that alcohol is suspected."

"I don't think so, but it's possible. I think it's more probable that he caught up to her. I want to get out of here. I don't even want a cookout anymore. I want to go… Shoot! I don't know where the safest place to be is!"

"Right now, I'd say anywhere but here." Arlie looked at the

boys. "Let's get them out of here ASAP."

Charlene took a swig of water, handed the bottle to Arlie, then picked up her backpack. "I'll walk ahead. If something bad happens, just grab my gun. I'll take the boys and run."

"Sounds like a plan, but I have my own gun." He lifted his pants leg, showing her his Glock G42. "You just grab the boys and go. I'd love a chance at payback to that ornery SOB, even if he hadn't killed Rosa. He shot me in cold blood and that kinda crap is too hard to forgive."

Carla looked over at the boys and called out, "Last one to the car is a rotten egg!" Then added, "But be careful and don't knock anyone off the trail or you immediately lose!"

The four of them scurried down the crushed granite trail, half-running, half-sliding in the steepest areas, always one of the adults leading the way, the other herding tail.

Half-way down, Carlos called out, "Arlie! Arlie! I gotta go pee. I don't think I can hold it any longer and I don't wanna pee my pants."

"Well, just go behind the bushes here. I'll wait for you."

"But it's not a bathroom…"

"Charlene, go on ahead. Carlos and I are going to water the bushes."

"Huh?" Carlos asked.

"Follow me." Arlie scouted out the area and found a suitable Palo Verde tree off the side of the trail with a stand of creosote bushes next to it. "You've never peed outside?"

"Nuh uh. My mamma and nannies never took me outside. We had a huge house, almost as big as Sprawl-Mart, and there was a garden, but if I had to pee, there were about a hundred bathrooms…" Carlos bent forward and groaned.

"Can you make it to that tree and those bushes?"

"Yeah," he said, then shuffled knock-kneed ahead of Arlie.

"Whoa, let me make sure…" *Don't scare the kid and tell them you're looking for snakes or murderers!* "Let me make a target for you," Arlie said, then bent a low twig on the yellow-blossomed bush. "Aim for that and you'll be fine. I'll watch and make sure no one's coming."

Arlie turned his back to Carlos, then scouted the area. He could hear the boy sigh in relief, his waterworks taking what seemed like forever.

"That was fun!" Carlos said when he was done. "And I didn't even have to remember to flush! Do guys get to do this all the time?"

"Yeah, we do, but only when we're outside and away from

a bathroom," he said. "Let's get back to Chip and Mommy.

Carlos suddenly squatted down. "Do you know what those are?" he asked. "They kinda look like chocolate candies."

Arlie squatted down beside him to check it out. "Nope, definitely not chocolate. That's rabbit poop…"

Eeeekkk!

Carlos and Arlie straightened up at Charlene's scream. "Go sit down on the other side of that tree. Don't come out unless I call you. This is like hide and seek, but not really a game. Do *not* come out unless Charlene or I call you. No one else. Do you understand?"

Arlie ushered the boy to a spot beside a manzanita bush, then bent down and took his Glock from his ankle holster and took off the safety.

I'll shoot him in cold blood if he hurts Charlene or Chip!

He looked back at Carlos. "And don't talk or make a noise, either. You're hiding, remember?"

Carlos nodded, then squatted down and hugged his knees. He'd hide and be quiet like his mama had taught him to when his father was angry, like he had to before they left Costa Rica.

Arlie ran to the noise, jumped over a large rock, then

cringed as his back spasmed on landing. *Not now! You can cripple me for the rest of my life, stupid bullet, just let me save the mother and son!*

Arlie's adrenaline kicked in and he never felt another twinge. When he found Charlene and Chip, dragged off the trail into a natural alley, his stomach knotted in his throat.

Luca had Charlene, paralyzed with a knife at her throat, and Alonzo had Chip by the shoulder, his grip so tight the boy was bent forward.

"That's not your son, Alonzo!" Arlie called out from the cover of a boulder.

The big swarthy Italian startled at being called by name. "Who are you? How do you know my name?"

"Your stink is hard to forget. Look again, asshole. That is not your son."

"If he was my *real* son, I wouldn't kill him, but this is..." Alonzo pulled the red hair back on the boy's forehead, suddenly unsure of the boy's identity. "How'd you get rid of that scar?"

Chip looked up at the scary man and now saw the other one had a knife to his mother's neck. "I don't have a scar there. Mine's here..." Chip wrestled away from the mustached man, twisted his right fist as if to indicate where a scar was, then punched Alonzo in the nuts. "Asshole!"

Chip ran to his mother's side, while Alonzo bent over double. "Chip!" Charlene cried, "Run the other way! Go to Arlie!"

Chip ran to where he had heard Arlie call the big mean man 'asshole.' Arlie gathered him close, then set him behind him. "Stay here and don't come out unless your mother or I call you," he said softly, then called out, "Let her go, Luca. She's nothing to you."

"Yeah, well except a ticket out of here. Who are you and how do you know my name?"

Arlie moved further down the trail and doubled back to the same side of the trail as Charlene. He scooted closer toward her, ignoring Luca's question so he didn't reveal his new location. He picked up a rock and threw it down the side of the trail.

Charlene felt Luca's hold lessen as he turned towards the sound, so twisted out of his grip. She picked up her fallen backpack, then swung it at the distracted man's head and ran to where Arlie had called out, her fist holding tight to the pack's strap.

"Mommy, Mommy," Chip cried out, "I'm over here!"

She rushed to his side, then scolded, "Shush," grabbing him under his arms and pulling him further away from the fracas, entrenching both of them behind a boulder off the trail. *Where were interfering people when you needed them?*

"But..." Chip protested.

Charlene clasped her hand over his mouth and shook her head.

He shook his head in reply and pointed up.

"Not as quick as you thought you were," Luca said, then reached for her.

Charlene ducked just in time, leaving Luca with nothing but a fistful of air.

"Come on," she said, and took Chip's arm, the two of them slipping and skidding down the steepest part of the sand and bedrock trail, scraping hands and fannies as they slid downhill, then sprinted to the picnic area.

Bang! Bang!

Two shots zinged past her ear, but she kept running. Great! Now that shots had been fired, someone was sure to call the cops or sheriff or someone!

Whoop! Whoop!

Two short blasts of a siren sounded off, letting her know where the sheriff was. She bundled up Chip and carried him in her arms like an infant to the other side of the official black and white vehicle.

"Are you all right, ma'am?" one of the officers asked.

"Just scraped up a bit, but my…my boyfriend and his son are up there. He's an Anchorage cop and two men are shooting at him. I hope the boy's still hidden, but the De Luca brothers are looking to kill him. And the father, too."

"The De Lucas are back? And they want to kill the boy or the father?"

"Both."

"Yeah. They're assholes," Chip said, then snorted.

"Chip!" Charlene scolded, then decided to let it ride. "They're up that trail. I don't know how many people are in the way, but it sure seems busy today."

The officer winced, then spoke into his shoulder-mounted radio. "Dispatch, we need a chopper with a gun up here. We have two suspects shooting on the Treasure Loop Trail at Lost Dutchman Park. It appears a man and a young boy are their targets. According to a witness, these are the De Luca brothers from Anchorage."

He was trapped, but by the sound of the siren, Abby had jumped the gun and called the sheriff's office right away. He really did love that gal. Only two shots had been fired. The law and their guns were here. And if by some chance Chip or Charlene had been hit, at least there was medical help nearby.

Now it was the waiting game. Crap! This was the hardest part.

"Carlos, come on out to Papa," Alonzo called in a falsetto voice. "Let's go see Mama. She misses you and wants you to come home with me…"

Alonzo strutted down the trail, calling out into the brush, hoping to bring in his wife's son. He chuckled softly. "My ex-wife's bastard son."

Suddenly, Carlos popped out from behind the bush Arlie had told him to stay behind. "She'd never tell me to come with you!" he shouted, then ran back toward the parking lot where he'd seen Charlene and Chip rush off to.

"Aha!" Alonzo said, then gave chase, shoving his hand gun in his shoulder holster.

Arlie thrust his revolver back in its holster. "Not on my

watch!" he hollered after Alonzo, then straight-arm shoved the bloated goon out of the way, speeding past him to grab Carlos. Arlie grabbed his son in his arms, then zig zagged down the trail, making sure he was a moving target rather than a stationary one.

Alonzo scrambled to his feet. "Gotcha!" he said, then pointed his gun at Arlie, grinning at besting the man who had put him behind bars. "I guess I figured out who the bastard was that knocked up Carla…"

Arlie kept moving, letting Alonzo's words fade into the cactus, dust, and brush. He knew not to hold still. By the look of sheer loathing he had seen on the thug's face, though, he didn't care if he spent the rest of his life in jail—he just wanted his 'honor' back.

"I got him," Luca called out to his brother. "It's either give up or jump, Daywalker. We just want the boy…"

Arlie glanced back and saw Alonzo was gaining on him. He could tell by Luca's voice that he was on the rise just ahead of him. The curve in the trail at his side provided a straight down, but unmarked shortcut to the main trail below. It was their only hope.

He jumped, skidding down the cactus-covered terrain, the

boy snuggled in front of him as he did his best to avoid the bigger patches of chollas and prickly pear cacti. He got to the trail below, gaining a hundred yards with the slice through the terrain, then felt the ping at the same time he heard the crack of the pistol.

Shot in the back.

Again.

He fell to his knees, then released Carlos from his arms. "Run!" he whispered hoarsely. "Run to Mommy…"

Carlos looked up and saw his father and uncle picking their way through the brush and cactus to where they were. "But…"

"Run to Mommy," he repeated, "son."

Carlos bolted, tears streaming down his face. His mother had told him that when they came to America, he'd never have to run from his father again, never have to hear him hurt someone he loved. Arlie wasn't his mother or any of his favorite nannies, and he wanted him safe. But he also knew he had to run.

***

Alonzo looked down at Daywalker, the man who had trapped him and his brother in the best money laundering scheme ever. The man was a genius at computers, but a dud when it came to taking a bribe. "You shoulda took the money, Daywalker," he said.

"Nah, it stunk too bad," Arlie said softly, then groaned. He didn't know which was worse, the new bullet in his back or the cactus thorns that covered him literally from head to toe. He realized that he could feel the prickles all up and down his legs and that meant he wasn't paralyzed. And both Alonzo and Luca were standing over him so Carlos had escaped. A sly smile crept across his face as he remembered what he had in his pocket.

"What's so damned funny?" Alonzo asked.

"Didn't you want to know about your wife and me?" Arlie whispered.

"No. Well, yeah. Sorta. I didn't know you even knew her."

"Come closer and I'll tell you…" Arlie said softly, coughing as if these were his last words, at the same time reaching into his pocket for the spare part from assembling Chip's bike.

Alonzo leaned down. He had taken the bait.

"Yeah…"

Arlie slammed the three-inch bolt into the man's ear, then

rolled away and pulled his Glock from his ankle holster. "Which one of you wants to die? I don't care which one or both. Just make a move and you'll fulfill my fantasy."

"I think we have it from here, Officer Biggar."

Arlie looked up and saw three deputies with weapons drawn, two on Luca, one on the writhing Alonzo, his hand covering the bolt that was still in his ear.

"Hey, Alonzo," Arlie said, then stifled a giggle. "Tell me if you've heard this one…" then rolled over laughing.

"You…you…" Alonzo sputtered, then stilled as one deputy nudged him with his boot.

"You have the right to remain silent…" the deputy said and began reading the De Luca brothers their rights.

"I need a stretcher down here," the sheriff called into his radio. "Gunshot victim plus looks like he's been rolled in cholla, then dipped in paddle cactus."

Chapter 11
Dipped in Glue and Stripped

The next morning
Banner Hospital

Helpful hint for new Arizonans: The best way to remove cactus spines and glochidia (the fine fuzzy cactus needles) is to first remove as many as you can with tweezers. Next, spread a layer of white glue (the kind used for many elementary school projects) onto the skin on top of the glochidia. Wait five minutes or until the glue has dried, then peel it off. Most of the prickles will be gone, but the irritation may remain for days. A topical corticosteroid will help alleviate the pain and itching.

***

"Well, Mr. Biggar, it looks as if the magnet in that back-support belt saved you from getting another bullet in the back." The doctor held up the half-inch thick by inch and a half round hardened magnet. "Look at that, would you? Almost dead center. Oh, and while we had you sedated, pulling out all those cactus needles, we got this out, too. Looks like that slug had worked its way to the surface. Just a little slit with the scalpel and I flicked it right out. If it was me,

I'd have these two framed and stuck on the wall."

"How about if I put them in a Christmas ornament and hang it on a tree?"

"Oh, your wife and boys are outside, eager to see you. I told them I had to finish covering you up. It's not that your wife hasn't seen that fanny of yours, but it might embarrass the boys."

"Can I talk to him alone for a minute, Doc?" Charlene asked as she stepped in.

"Sure. Come into this room here, boys," he said and ushered the boys away, "And I'll let you listen to your heart."

"Well, Arlie, you may not have had freckles before, but it looks like you have them now," Charlene said. "Here, look." She handed him the compact she had pulled out of her purse. "Keep the mirror. I think it's going to be a few days before you can sit down or be on your back."

He looked in it, groaned, then closed it.

"What about Rosa? Did you have a talk with Carlos?" he asked, craning his neck so he could see her.

"Yes, Carlos and I talked, and Child Protection Services and I talked, and the police and I talked, and Abby and I talked..."

Arlie hung his head down, then opened the mirror so he could see her face. "And..."

"Carlos can stay with me. No problem there unless you want to ask for a paternity test and take him away. I figured you and I could work something out later about that, but since you're in no shape to take care of anyone—even yourself—for a few days, I figured it was best to keep my mouth shut and let them think that his mother was dead and father in custody for her murder."

"And the police?"

"Alonzo and Luca will have to stay here until the authorities are done, as they say, throwing the book at them. Alonzo's probably going to be deaf in one ear, but no one's pressing charges against you. It was a clear case of self-defense. 'Armed with a three-inch bolt, Anchorage Police Officer Charles Biggar escapes death in the Arizona desert.'"

"Wait... Where was that?"

"Hmph. That's where the conversation with Abby comes in. I guess she made a mock up newspaper and sent it around. You'll be getting a copy of it in a day or so, after she's got all the get well wishes added to it. Oh, and she says to say thanks for the picture you sent of your family."

"Yeah, I sent her one of the photos we took at the top of the hill. Anything else interesting?"

"Oh, yeah… It gets better and better. I almost think Santa heard us. All we're missing is the Stingray bicycle."

"Come here a minute," he said. She knelt down next to his face. "I'm storing it for him in my bedroom. That's where the spare part came from."

"Oh! Cool!" she said and stood up again. "By the way, I took the liberty of telling HR that you were in an accident and were in the hospital. I didn't quit your job for you, but just know you're covered for a week."

Charlene walked over to the big picture window. "You may get your wish for a white Christmas, too. A winter storm is coming this way. We may or may not get snow down here in the Valley, but it's pretty much a sure thing for the Stupidstious, I mean Superstition Mountains by Christmas morning."

"Thanks for covering my ass, at least the HR part," Arlie said, tugging on the sheet that had slipped off his fanny. "And a white Christmas? The boys will go nuts! Where are they, anyhow?"

"Not yet. Like I said, it keeps getting better. The cops let us in Rosa's house after they had checked it for clues. Since the rent was paid up for a year and Carlos was listed on the lease, it looks like we have new digs!"

"Great! Looks like you won't be moving to an extra dry spot in the desert without electricity for a while."

"Well, I could if I—or Carlos and his new family—wanted to. You see, Carlos showed me the where the big bag of dog food was where Rosa kept her money. It was still there! On top of the three-foot tall bag of hundred-dollar bills was a hand-written note saying that if anything should happen to her, that I was to take care of Carlos, and this money was for me to use as I saw fit to help him grow into a good man."

Arlie dropped his hand and brought his head up. "You're shitting me!"

"Where did that phrase come from? No, I'm not shitting you. Not only do we have a big house to live in—rent-free for a year—we're rich!"

Arlie's head slumped back into the bed. *So now if you ask her to marry you, she'll think you're after her money.*

"Arlie, are you all right? I thought you'd be happy."

"Yes, I'm happy for you and the boys. I guess I just have a sedative hangover or something. What have the boys been up to?"

"Well, they asked me to write letters to Santa for them. They said they'd sign their names so Santa knew it was really from them. They're both very proud that they can do that now.

"Carlos said he wanted a brother. He said he was sad that his mother was dead, but he'd give Santa everything he had—all the money Mama had hidden and even his Stingray bike—if he could have a brother. Then he looked at Chip. But it had to be a brother who looked just like him and whose name was Chip. It was a long request, but I told him I wrote it in shorthand.

"Chip said he wanted a Stingray bicycle. No surprise there. Then he said he really, really wanted that bike, but he'd rather have a daddy. But he said it had to be Arlie. Then he asked me if that would be okay." Charlene grinned, then sighed.

"Of course, not to be outdone in the huge requests from Santa department, Carlos said he wanted a daddy, too. But he had to look just like him. And his name had to be Arlie, too."

"And, and..." Arlie prompted, not even trying to hide his

exasperation. "Well, if you aren't going to tell me what you told Chip, would you at least tell me what *you* asked Santa for?"

"I told him I wanted a daddy for my boys. But it couldn't be any man. He had to have red hair and brown eyes like my boys which, as you know, is an uncommon trait. Oh, and he had to be named Arlie."

The doctor knocked on the door. "Can I bring them in now? I have to take a call."

"Oh, yes, doctor. Thank you so much," Charlene said, then ushered the boys in the room.

"He's going to be okay but has to lie on his belly for a few days until the cactus owies are healed."

"Can I tell him now?" Chip asked.

"Tell him what?"

Chip squatted down on the floor in front of Arlie and looked up at him. "Mommy said we weren't allowed to come in and see you unless you were our daddy, so for today, you're my daddy. Can you be my daddy tomorrow, too?" he asked.

Carlos got down on the floor and scooted next to Chip. "Mine, too?" he asked.

"Today, tomorrow, forever as far as I'm concerned. That is, as long as it's all right with Mommy."

"If that's a proposal, I accept. If it's not, well, hurry up, Christmas! Maybe Santa will make my wish come true."

Arlie rose up on his elbows, stifling the grunt of discomfort. "Yes, that's a proposal. You'll just have to wait a few days before I get on bended knee."

"Well, I've waited nearly six years for a father for my son, I can wait a few more days."

"No, I was already the father. I want to be their daddy."

"So, you're our real daddy now?" Chip asked.

"Our really daddy?" Carlos echoed.

"Your daddy forever and ever."

Arlie relaxed back into the bed. *And now that the bullet is out of your back, you can have intimate relations again!*

"Charlene, one question. How do you feel about having more children…the old-fashioned way?"

"Well, I've always wanted a daughter…"

The End

THANK YOU!

Thanks for reading *A Stingray Christmas*, first book in the *Arlie Undercover* series. If you'd like a chance at getting an ARC (advanced readers copy) of my upcoming books or find out random (and hopefully interesting) information, please sign up for Time Travelers Anonymous. I promise I won't plug up your inbox with loads of newsletters and I will not share your contact information with any other person or site. http://bit.ly/dhNewsltr

About the Author

Dani Haviland, a Mayflower descendant born in Connecticut, has spent most of her life living in Arizona and Alaska. She semi-retired from selling tractors and roses in Alaska and now spends her time with writing, gardening, and taking pictures, sometimes incorporating all of them in a single project. *A Stingray Christmas* is the first book in the new *Arlie Undercover* romantic suspense series. More of her stories in *The Fairies Saga* are still in the works, too. Sometimes it's good to have a bit of Attention Deficit Disorder!

Other books by Dani Haviland

Naked in the Winter Wind: It all began with a tumble back in time where 'Evie' became involved with the fictional characters of a popular romance novel. A bottle of Fountain of Youth water, amnesia, abandonment, and adoptions complicated her new life in Revolutionary War era North Carolina. But the men were hot and the women tough. First appearance of Jenny and Scout in the series

Ha'Penny Jenny (Historical novella) A bit more about our young lady and her new family.

Aye, I am a Fairy: He's not what she thinks he is, but he can help her in her time travel dilemma. Lots about James and Leah, Scout and Jenny in this one.

Dances Naked: Directionally challenged British lord is trying to get back to his family in the 21st century when he is found by a Cherokee hunting party. What will it take to get the chief to lead him to the Trees, the portal through time?

Little Bear and the Ladies (Historical novella) The gentle 18th century trapper we first met in NITWW steps in to save the day for the survivors. Now what's he going to do with so many women?

The Great Big Fairy: Benji finally returns to his

grandparents in the 18th century, but he didn't plan on acquiring a very strong, and stubborn, female slave who can't—or won't—speak.

Chasing Christmas: (Historical novella) This is where the novella you just read comes in chronologically. Jenny, Scout, and many more have a very unexpected surprise during the holiday season.

Little Drummer Boy (Historical novella) Young Scout wants to earn money as a scout but is told he's only good enough to be a drummer boy. Can he help the others find their way during one of the worst snowstorms of the 18th century?

Never Too Young (Historical novella) Scout is older now, and managed to earn enough to return to Jenny and provide her with a proper home, but will a con artist ruin his plans? And after the long separation, will she still be waiting for him?

Pool Boy Wanted: No Experience Preferred (a rather racy novella) Young Benji would do anything to save his friend, and she knew it. Bad cougar!

Luke the Unexpected Luke wanted to get the attention of the hot blonde who loved vintage motorcycles. Occurs right after **Pool Boy Wanted: No Experience Preferred.**

Time in a Little Blue Bottle (contemporary romance fantasy mash up) Can the young woman and teenage pickpocket beat Elvis and Mark Twain to the Fountain of Youth elixir? And whose side is the vampire on?

Kit Kringle: An Alaskan Tale (contemporary novella) Falling in love was not part of her business plan

Be My Angel (contemporary novella) Wyatt's dream to help save the wild horses in the west started with buying a rundown ranch in western Oregon. What he hadn't anticipated was being mesmerized by a sassy woman in a wheelchair.

Three Are One (contemporary novella) The post chaplain tried to help the young widow adjust but would his feelings for her and search for his lost sister get in the way?

One Arctic Summer (contemporary novella) Barrow, Alaska, 1994: The touch she never forgot.

Arlie Undercover Series

A Stingray Christmas: (First book in the Arlie Undercover series) Anchorage detective on medical leave travels from Alaska to Arizona to see for the first time the son he'd fathered as an anonymous sperm donor. Great and rotten surprises await the cop with the smartest smartphone around.

The Biggest Heart Ever: (Book two in the Arlie Undercover series) When would Arlie learn that trying to do everything by himself could be deadly—and make Charlene a widow before they were married?

Always a Bigger Fish: (Book three in the Arlie Undercover series) Back in Alaska, Arlie finds out he's a target. Will vacationing detective Billy Burke (from THE FAIRIES SAGA) have information to help nab the scalper?

CONTACT INFO:

Website: www.danihaviland.com

https://www.facebook.com/dani.haviland

Amazon Author page: http://bit.ly/dhAuthor

Twitter: @dani_haviland

Book Bub Author page: http://bit.ly/BBDani

Goodreads: http://bit.ly/2DHgdrds

Email: dani@danihaviland.com

Blog: http://bit.ly/DHbLog

www.ingramcontent.com/pod-product-compliance
Lightning Source LLC
Chambersburg PA
CBHW082010170626
46817CB00009B/3051